A LETHAL BETRAYAL

A RITCHIE AND FITZ SCI-FI MURDER MYSTERY

KATE MACLEOD

1

MURDINA RITCHIE PRESSED her face close to the thick shuttle window, mindless of the deep chill from space that still radiated through the double-paned glass. They were only just entering the atmosphere of her homeworld of Buennagel. No details were yet discernible beyond the wisps of high clouds that streaked past the window as they descended. But she could feel her heart beating in her throat.

She hadn't seen this place in years. She had dreamt of it often, but with the clouds obscuring everything, she felt a sudden, irrational fear that her memories of the planet below were all wrong. That she only remembered the dream version and not the real one.

She couldn't articulate why that mattered, but it did. And the fear was real enough that her hands were clammy, sweating despite the cold air so close to the window.

She would be more comfortable if she took just half a step back. The climate-controlled environment inside the shuttle was set to a level where she and her friends were almost too warm in their Oymyakon Foreign Service Academy uniforms. But even the warmth of the air aside, her mug of sweet, lemony tea was waiting for her back at her seat. The salty, tamari smell of whatever Shackleton Fitz IV—whose family shuttle they were traveling in—had dialed up for lunch was inviting enough to set her stomach to growling.

But sampling either the tea or the tamari dish meant stepping away from the window. And at the moment, she couldn't even force herself to lift her forehead away from the glass.

Finally, the last wisps of cloud parted all at once, and the expanse of prairie that suddenly appeared below her was so verdantly green she sucked in a breath.

The rolling hills, the smudges of purple and yellow flower meadows that dotted the never-ending grass, it was all exactly as she remembered it.

There was a burst of static from the speaker just over her head, and the voice of the pilot crackled on. "We'll be landing in ten. Stow all loose items and belt in."

Ritchie left the window with a sigh and headed back to her seat. She reached for her tea, but the mug was gone. Then she looked up to see her petite, blonde buddy Antoinette Moreau give her a little wave gesture with the cup she was holding in her hand. Ritchie nodded her thanks.

As she buckled in, she saw that Fitz's buddy Kristof Wyss sitting across from her already had his belt fastened. She wondered if he had ever even taken it off since they left Oymyakon the day before. His pale blonde head had been bent over his tablet every time she had looked his way.

Tassa Sokolov beside him was also buckled in and ready for landing. But Ritchie couldn't see her face—turned as it was towards Fitz on the other side of the aisle—only the back of her head where the long coils of her chestnut braid-crown met each other neatly at her nape. She flopped back against her seat with a sigh, then realized Ritchie was looking at her. She shrugged, then tipped her head towards Fitz and shrugged again.

Ritchie didn't know what all that meant, but then she looked over at Fitz sitting by himself on the far side of the aisle. His bowl of food was still on the table in front of him, despite the pilot's words. He didn't seem to be aware of it. Not the food, or the pilot, or anything. He just stared off into space, biting at his thumbnail absentmindedly as one of his knees bounced rapidly up and down.

"Did you want to finish?" Moreau asked him as she reached for his bowl.

"What? No. It's fine," Fitz said. But automatically, like even when she had touched his shoulder, he hadn't really heard what she said.

Ritchie knew that Fitz got stressed out anytime he was in the presence of his father, but after a very awkward hello to all of them collectively at the landing site back on Oymyakon, his father hadn't left the cockpit even once, and Fitz hadn't gone up to talk with him. Was he worried about what would happen when they landed?

Or was he worried about their mission? The few hurried words that Colonel Hansen had exchanged with them just before Fitz's father's shuttle had landed hadn't made a lot of sense. But Ritchie gathered the gist of it was they were going to meet a contact while they were on Buennagel, someone who needed to remain secret. Someone who could never meet with them on Oymyakon. Ritchie didn't know any more than that, but she sensed that Fitz did.

"Are you worried about finding our contact?" Ritchie asked him.

"What?" Fitz asked, snapping up as if she had woken him from his fugue state. His hand dropped away from his mouth and his knee finally fell still.

"You seem… preoccupied," she said. "Do you know who we're supposed to meet? Or what they're like?"

"No, not really," Fitz said, glancing up at Moreau as she finally took the seat beside him and buckled in.

"I wouldn't worry too much about first impressions," Moreau said. "Colonel Hansen seemed scary and intense when we first met him, right? And now, he's…" She trailed off, unable to find the words.

"He's Colonel Hansen," Fitz finished for her.

"Scary and intense," Ritchie said. "But on our side."

"But meeting our contact is only item number two on Fitz's to-do list," Moreau said, and turned to give Fitz a fixed look. "Isn't it?"

"Yeah," Fitz said glumly.

He had promised to finally tell Ritchie the truth. Whatever he had been hiding from her. But not yet. Not on the shuttle.

Ritchie pushed all thoughts of it aside before those thoughts could start driving her mad again.

Then the pilot's voice started murmuring to them, his words lost in the roar of the engines as the shuttle dropped down to land.

They banked sharply, spiraling in like a leaf on the wind. She wished she could still watch through the window as the grasslands and flowers of home finally grew close enough to make out real details, but all she could see through the glass from her seat was the indigo blue of the sky.

She sucked in a breath again. She had forgotten just how blue the skies of Buennagel were. How could she have forgotten that? How many afternoons had she spent sprawled on her back looking up at that sky and wishing she could be up in it?

She glanced up at Fitz, and he gave her a little smile, like he had just been having the same memory too.

Then the shuttle set softly down on the platform and the engines cut off. The pilot remotely opened the side door, and the sounds of home rushed in to meet them. The wind whispering through the grass, the buzz of countless bees, the drone of the cicadas.

And with the sound came the warmth of the wind, and with the wind came the familiar smells. The dry smell of the grass. The sweet smell of the flowers. And the strongest of those was the honey smell of the Immerweis.

The Immerweis only bloomed once a year for five days. During those five days, the air was thick with their aroma. And after those five days, the smell was even stronger as the people of Buennagel cooked down the harvested blossoms into a thick syrup they cherished for the rest of the year until the Immerweis bloomed again.

She had forgotten that smell, too. She had forgotten helping her mother with the still, condensing armful after armful of faded blossoms into a single jar of golden syrup. And once that jar was full, whatever was left in the still, her mother used to make the candy that was known as Maiden's Breath. Only faintly sweet as it melted on your tongue, but that sweetness lingered for hours afterward.

How had she forgotten it?

And would they be staying long enough for the harvest and distilling days? Would she have a chance to taste that candy again?

She was the last to unbuckle from her seat and just barely caught her duffle bag as Moreau tossed it to her. So barely caught it that for a second she thought it would continue past her, her fingertips gripping the corner so tenuously.

But someone behind her kept it from sailing past her. Thinking it was Fitz, she turned to thank him and found herself looking up at Fitz's father, General Shackleton Fitz III.

And he was glowering down at her, putting the duffle back into her arms with a shove. She had avoided him as they boarded the shuttle, and since he hadn't come back to the cabin once during the whole voyage, she had managed to avoid him for all of that day. But she was face to face with him now.

And it was clear his feelings for her were not changed.

Was this a mistake? Fitz had wanted her to be here with him. She had thought over all the reasons not to come, but never spoke them aloud. There were so many memories to confront here, but she had decided that if Fitz needed her, she could handle confronting her past.

What she hadn't taken into account was all the time she was going to be in the company of his father. A man she suspected had actively thwarted her academic career on more than one occasion. A man who had exerted great influence in his quest to keep his son and her far apart.

He had failed at both, but that only made her fear him more. What more would he do? And what if he succeeded?

Yes, this was feeling more and more like a mistake. Especially the idea of being a guest under his roof.

"Is my father's house still standing?" Ritchie asked. Her voice sounded so small, not how she had wanted to project herself at all.

Fitz's father just gave her a puzzled frown, like he wasn't sure what language she was speaking.

"It's still there, but it's occupied by the current diplomat in residence, of course," Fitz told her. "Were you hoping to see it?"

She was hoping to stay in it, but clearly that wasn't going to be how this went at all. She just shrugged.

But the general was still staring down at her with that glowering look. Like she was a puzzle to him, yes, but that it was a puzzle that was angering him. A lot.

Then another man in a military uniform came into the cabin from the cockpit. Ritchie couldn't remember his name, but she gathered he was Fitz's father's aide-de-camp. There was something about the inky blackness of his hair or in the way his dark eyes were just a shade too close together that made her feel uneasy. Or maybe it was the way he moved, like he was always slinking about. He slid up to the general's elbow and murmured something brief but inaudible close to his ear.

"Fitz, lead your friends up to the house, will you?" his father said. He didn't wait for an answer, just swept down the ramp with that man half a step behind him.

"That guy creeps me out," Ritchie whispered when she was sure they were out of earshot.

"You mean Klemm? Tell me about it," Fitz said, his voice also pitched low. "He's always quietly there. It's annoying. My father has never had an assistant who had no concept of family time the way this guy does."

"Maybe he's a spy," Moreau said, raising her eyebrows as if the thought tickled her. "Maybe he's our contact. Who's also a spy. Spying on your dad."

"I don't think so," Fitz said.

"He fits the scary and intense profile," Sokolov said.

"Yeah, but you don't know my father the way I do," Fitz said. "There's no way that guy is a spy and my father doesn't know about it. And if he knew about it, he'd be gone. I won't deny he's creepy, but I think it's a harmless sort of creepy."

"I hope so," Ritchie said. "This whole trip is going to be stressful enough without being constantly observed by that guy."

"He watched us the whole time we were at the townhouse on Jorda," Wyss said. "I think you better steel yourself to the idea of being watched, Ritchie."

"Let's get up to the house," Fitz said, gesturing for the others to precede him down the ramp. "I want to catch a moment alone with my father before dinner, and the sooner the better."

Ritchie wanted to drag her feet. The shuttle suddenly felt like her safe space, and she was loath to leave it.

But there was something in Fitz's brown eyes when he looked at her. Some eager expectation. Whatever he wanted to talk to his father about, he was very keyed up about it. And she got the sense that he wanted to share it with her, later.

That was a lot to fit in before dinner.

But the thought of dinner hit another dread spot in her mind. "Is this going to be a formal dinner?" she asked, biting at her lip in anticipation of what she already knew was going to be the answer.

"At my house? There isn't any other kind," Fitz said.

She was afraid of that.

But then Moreau slipped her hand into Ritchie's and gave it a squeeze before leading her down the ramp, out into the sunshine and the flower-scented wind.

Ritchie was where she never thought she'd be again.

Home.

2

SHACKLETON FITZ IV was back in his father's office on Buennagel for the first time in half a decade, and it hadn't changed a bit.

And it really should have. Or it should feel different because he was different. But it didn't.

He still felt incredibly small. Like his feet didn't quite touch the floor as he sat deep inside the leathery embrace of the chair that was always positioned across from his father's own at the massive stone desk.

Yes, stone. It came up out of the floor, emerging from the flagstones like some sort of monster out of a primordial ooze. The surface was a computer screen, of course, but the privacy settings didn't allow Fitz on the other side of the desk to see any of it. From where he sat, it looked like his father was just very interested in the patterns of the stone surface before him, flicking at one before staring intently at another.

The walls around him were stone too, and extended up into the second story in order to contain the enormous number of books his father owned. Actual printed books from all over the Union of the Free Worlds and beyond. Some of them were priceless artifacts, others were a collector's personal amusements, but they were all shelved together according to some scheme known only to his father, the general.

And all the shelves were stone as well. The black- and white-flecked grayness of all that stone seemed to smother even the brightest of book spines. It was oppressive.

And cold.

Fitz tucked his nose down into the collar of his uniform tunic, not so much to warm it as to get another sniff of the prairie smell he had brought in with him from outside. The warm smell of the grass was soothing. The syrupy sweet smell of the Immerweis was nearly too overwhelming. It almost made him dizzy.

But he remembered the Maiden's Breath Ritchie's mother had made every harvest time. It had been divine, like putting a bit of a magic cloud on your tongue and letting it melt away. He wondered if Ritchie remembered that candy. He doubted her mother had been able to make it again after leaving Buennagel for the space station on the far side of the Union. Maybe she had forgotten.

He hoped not. He hoped she knew the recipe. If they were here just a few extra days, they could distill some of the syrup themselves and make a batch of that candy.

If she was still speaking to him when this was all over, that was.

Ritchie had been withdrawn the entire shuttle flight from Oymyakon. He knew she was wrestling with a lot of emotions, but she wasn't letting a single one of them show. He wanted to ask how she was doing. What she was feeling and what she was thinking. But he couldn't. That wall was still between them, the one he had erected himself to protect her.

He was so close to being able to tear it down, but he wasn't there yet. So he had had to watch from a distance as Ritchie kept a tight clasp on Moreau's hand all during the short walk from the shuttle landing platform on one of the higher rolling hills of their childhood home to the enormous edifice where his family dwelt.

His father was a general in the Union of Free Worlds military, but he was also the governor of Buennagel. Because of that, Fitz had never known a home in the sense that Ritchie had: an enclosed space just for one family. No, what he had was a bedroom in the set-off parts of an administrative building. The dining room, the kitchens, the library, the so-called living room, were all public places. Local people coming to petition his father, travelers stopping by on their way between systems, or other military officers on official business, all mingled together in those places.

He had been nervous as he and his fellow cadets left the path through the grasslands behind to cross the gravel court to the massive, open front doors into the greeting hall that they wouldn't understand the distinctions between public and private, but he quickly realized they got it just fine.

Ritchie had been here often enough as a child to understand it intuitively. Moreau had enough friends who were children of politicians and public officials to have been in just such a place many times. Wyss had spent a semester break with Fitz at his family's townhouse on the UFW capital planet of Jorda, a space only slightly more homey than here due to his father having a separate office in the military headquarters.

Sokolov was the only one he should've really been worried about, but even she seemed to grasp the double-purpose of the building at once. But then again, she had worked the VIP cars of the Intergalactic Railway long enough to know how the upper crust lived.

So they had all stayed in a tight cluster around him, waiting for a cue from him where they should go next.

But he had needed to get to his father's office as soon as possible. So he had foisted them off on one of the security officials, even going so far as to make one of the guards carry his bag up to his room.

And he really needn't have bothered. Rushing to get here had been a waste of effort. The chronometer in the corner of his field of vision kept ticking away, the better part of an hour, and still he was being ignored.

Fitz sighed and sat up straighter in the over-sized chair, hoping to catch his father's eye. But his father was intent on only two things: the screens in front of him that Fitz could not see, and the whispers of Lieutenant Florus Klemm in his ear.

Klemm could see the screens. Of course he could. Klemm could see everything. But what did he do with what he saw?

Was Moreau right? Could he be a spy?

But sent by who?

"There. That's the worst of it caught up with," Fitz's father said, sitting back from his desk before pressing his thumb down on the security lock to shut it all down.

"Great! I was hoping—" Fitz began, but Klemm spoke right over him, as if he wasn't even there.

"There is the matter of the dinner this evening, sir," Klemm said, sliding one tablet into a side pocket of his uniform pants before taking out another from the opposite pocket and tapping it to life.

"Luana has it all in hand, surely," Fitz's father said, rubbing tiredly at his eyes.

"The dinner itself, of course, sir," Klemm said. "But we still need to go over the review materials I've prepared on all the various factions who will be attending. It is a rather large affair this time."

"Bad timing," Fitz's father grumbled. Then he glanced up, just for a second, almost at Fitz.

"Father, I really wanted to—" Fitz said, all in a rush. But he still wasn't fast enough. Klemm spoke over him again.

"There is an audio-visual element to the materials, sir," Klemm said. "Perhaps we should adjourn to the secure briefing room?"

"Of course," Fitz's father said, and got up from this chair. He looked tired in a way that Fitz had never seen him before. As if the flight to Oymyakon and back had taken everything out of him.

Which made no sense. His father flitted around the Union of Free Worlds constantly. He was seldom stationed in any one location for long, and even when technically stationed somewhere, his job still kept him on the move. So what was making him so tired now?

"Father," Fitz said again. He had to repeat it twice more, the last time almost at a shout, before his father finally turned to acknowledge him. Klemm had made it all the way out to the hall but came back to see what was delaying the general. He gave Fitz a cold glare of unspoken reprimand, but Fitz could not care less what Klemm thought of him.

"Fitz, yes," his father said, for all the world like he really hadn't realized his son was there the entire time. The son he had just spent days traveling to pick up and bring home. Not at Fitz's request, not at all. No, because he had been all fired up about something.

Like Fitz violating his parole while under arrest for a crime he hadn't committed was upsetting enough to demand his personal attention, the job of generaling or whatever be damned.

"Father, I just—" Fitz began, but this time it was his father that interrupted him.

"Fitz, I *do* want to talk with you, but this is not the time," he said.

"Well, when is the time?" Fitz asked, his irritation plain. "You're the one who demanded I leave Oymyakon and come back here with you. But you've never said why."

"You know what you did," his father said, narrowing his eyes warningly at him.

"I know what I did, but I also know what I didn't do," Fitz said. "And so do you."

"Sir, we really don't have the time for this," Klemm said. It was meant to be a whisper close to his boss's ear, but it was pitched to carry. He wanted Fitz to hear.

"Quite right," the general said.

"You're not even going to ask what I mean?" Fitz demanded. "Because I wasn't talking about violating my parole or being a suspect in a murder. That's not the 'what I did and didn't do' I'm referring to."

"I'm sure this is a very important family matter," Klemm said, but the disdain dripping from his words undercut their meaning quite a bit.

"It is," the general said to him brusquely. But then he turned back to Fitz. "This isn't the time."

"How is it not the time? You literally pulled me out of school to be here with you. So, please, let's get this over with."

His father said nothing. The stoniness of his face made the decor of his office feel soft by comparison.

But then something changed. The corners of his eyes scrunched up, the hard line of his mouth loosened. Something subtle like that. But Fitz felt it more than saw it, anyway.

For just a flash, he knew his father was deeply filled with sorrow. But for what?

Before he could delve deeper or even think to ask, Klemm was speaking again. "Sir?"

"Yes, quite," his father said, and his face was back to stony, barely contained anger in the blink of an eye.

"Come on, father," Fitz pleaded. He had to squash down all the irritation he was feeling at his father and at Klemm both. He had to keep his tone respectful. It was his only chance of being heard. "Can't you just send Klemm into the briefing room to set up? I only need a minute."

That absolutely wasn't true. He knew what he had to say, let alone what his father would have to say in response, was going to take far longer than a minute. But all he needed was a minute to suck his father in so deep, not even Klemm could pull him away. Not until every word was said.

The stony expression on his father's face didn't soften this time, but he was thinking. Fitz could see the thoughts firing behind those dark eyes. He was going to say yes.

But, of course, Klemm had to butt in one last time.

"We have less than an hour before the pre-dinner gathering, sir," Klemm said.

"Can't you just stuff it? For five minutes?" Fitz snapped at him.

He wished he could take those words back, even before he saw the anger in his father's eyes.

"Is that really how you address a superior officer, cadet?" the general growled at him.

"We're in our home, father," Fitz said, still surly if not outright venomous.

"You're in uniform, cadet," the general said.

Fitz said nothing. But the sullen silence stretched on too long. It was just too intolerable, being stuck there under that angry glare.

"Lieutenant Klemm, I apologize for my words. They were inappropriate," he said. Then, far too late, remembered to add, "sir."

"Apology accepted," Klemm said impatiently. "Sir, we really must get going."

"Of course," Fitz's father said. "Fitz, I shall see you at dinner. I expect you and your fellow cadets to be on your best behavior. It's disappointing I should even feel like I have to tell you that, but perhaps I shouldn't be surprised. You showed me your true colors years ago, and fool that I am, I keep thinking our fine foreign service academies will change you."

"Yes, sir," Fitz said, swallowing miserably.

"Behave. For your mother's sake, if not for mine," his father said.

And then he was gone, and Fitz was alone in the cavernous stone cave of his father's office. And he felt very small indeed.

3

RITCHIE LOOKED around the bedroom she was sharing with Moreau, walking with her hands carefully folded behind her back lest she be tempted to touch something.

She knew everything she saw was some sort of antique, priceless and irreplaceable. The room was large and comfortable, the entire eastern wall nothing but opened glass doors that let in the warm afternoon air. Even all the way up here on the fourteenth floor, she could smell the grass and flowers. Strangely, the Immerweis were more muted, though. Perhaps whatever carried its scent was just too heavy to extend up so far.

But she decided that was a good thing. She had just emerged from the shower, and the warm breeze dancing through her curls was drying her hair for her. The grass and drier-smelling flowers would leave their scent behind, but not the far too perfumey Immerweis.

She could hear Moreau singing something through the closed bathroom door and smiled to herself as she moved from examining a strange sort of sculpture that felt more like a work of science than one of art to a display of weapons. She had rushed her own shower, too used to the constant need to hurry that was her daily life back at the

Oymyakon Foreign Service Academy. But Moreau never missed an opportunity to relax and enjoy things.

Moreau's song ended mid-syllable. Then the water cut off and the shower door clicked open. Ritchie accessed her implant and saw a message from Fitz calling them all to meet him in his sitting room. Out of what was fast becoming a habit, she made sure all of her implant's settings were still on the lowest intrusion levels before shifting her awareness back to the wall in front of her.

No more constant mapping of the world around her, no more constant display of the current time in the corner of her vision, no more instant notification of any and all messages. Not for her. Her implant had been used against her far too many times. If she could remove it without tanking any possible future career, she would. Not even Wyss, who understood everything he studied, could explain why her implant had been used against her again and again. And he couldn't promise there was a way to make it safe.

She took a deep breath and forced her attention back to the weapons on the wall, away from anxieties she couldn't fight. It looked like all three weapons were of a set: a long, curved sword; a shorter straight sword, and a knife curved so strongly it looked more like a scythe. The scabbards had repeating patterns worked into the leather, although age had worn away so much of the color that she couldn't make out just what the patterns were.

She was just reaching out to touch that knife handle, to turn it at a better angle to the light behind her, when Moreau came into the room already dressed in her formal uniform, although she had left her hair down.

"Fitz wants us," Moreau told her as she went to her bed and dug through her duffle bag for her brush.

"I saw that," Ritchie said. "He didn't say what about, though."

"Yeah, I noticed that too," Moreau said with a frown. She stopped brushing her hair in mid-stroke, lost in thought for a moment, before resuming.

"What?" Ritchie asked.

"Nothing," Moreau said. Then, before Ritchie could press, said, "were you ever up here as a kid?" She was walking backwards, through the wind-spun lengths of sheer curtain, to the balcony beyond.

"Of course," Ritchie said, following her out into the afternoon light. She pointed to where their balcony was separated from the next by a low wall. "Those are Fitz's rooms, just there. I spent a lot of time up here. Although Fitz always preferred to be at my house."

"Can you see your house from here?" Moreau asked, still brushing her hair, not bothered by the way the wind kept carrying it away from her.

"No, it's on the other side, and there are several hills between," Ritchie said, leaning her elbows on the balcony wall to look down at the prairie. "I know it looks flat from up here, but it really isn't."

"I'm sure we'll get to visit your house before we go," Moreau said, gathering her hair up into a topknot, then going back into the room to put her brush away.

"I'm not sure that's relevant to why we're here," Ritchie said. There may have been an edge of sarcasm to her tone, but she couldn't help the irony. She knew there was more than one reason they were here. She just didn't know what the other reason was. Not yet. And she wouldn't put it past Fitz to decide again that he just couldn't talk to her, no matter what he had said before.

"Come on," Moreau said, braiding the long tail of her topknot even as she headed for the door. Ritchie ran to open it for her, then followed Moreau out into the sunless stillness of the corridor. Sokolov was just emerging from her own room a little further down the corridor. She smiled and quickened her steps to join them in the short walk to Fitz's rooms.

"Do you know what this is about?" Sokolov asked.

"Not a clue," Ritchie said. "I get the feeling he wanted to go over something before dinner, though. Hence the timing."

"Makes sense," Sokolov agreed.

Moreau finished wrapping the braid around her topknot with a little pat, then knocked once on the door at the end of the corridor before just turning the handle and letting them all inside.

The room beyond extended across the entire building from east to west, and doors on both sides were open to let the breezes through. The floor was a stone tile, but she knew from experience it would feel warm under bare feet even when not bathing in the sunlight.

When she had first come into this room as a little girl, it had been stuffed full of toys. Slowly, over the years, blocks and climbing structures had become models of military vehicles and tables covered with miniatures and figurines for all the thousand games she and Fitz had once played together. Shortly before she had seen it last, it had been changing again, the models and military tabletop games disappearing in favor of a video game system and chairs comfortable enough to game in.

But now even that was gone. Now, it was just a sitting area, like a living room, but without the sense of a family ever spending time in here. Ritchie had no clue who had picked out the furniture, but the utilitarian tables and the padded but not too comfortable sofas felt more like they belonged in one of the public rooms downstairs than something that should be part of a teenaged boy's personal space.

But then again, Ritchie doubted Fitz ever spent much time here, if at all. The last few semester breaks, he had joined his parents not here but at other places where his father was stationed. She even wondered if this was his first time seeing the changes himself.

"Good, you're here," Fitz said as he materialized in front of the three of them, a tray of tall drinks in his hands.

"What's this?" Sokolov asked brightly, choosing one of the three frosted glasses.

"Just lemon water, nothing fancy," Fitz said. "If we filled up before dinner, my mother would have a fit."

"Wyss is already here, I see," Moreau said, taking a glass of her own, then gliding across the stone tile floor to settle onto the sofa beside Wyss. He wasn't looking at a tablet this time, but only because he had an entire computer system balanced on his knees. He was so focused on whatever he was doing, he didn't even notice Moreau joining him.

"What're we doing?" Ritchie asked, taking the last of the glasses and sipping at the lemon water. There was more to it than that, she could tell. A hint of mint, and something sweet. But the hydrating citrus was the top note. She hadn't realized how thirsty she was until it hit her tongue.

She realized Fitz was looking at her. Yet again she had the strong feeling that he was five seconds away from telling her something, but after she counted to ten, he still hadn't spoken. Instead, he dropped his eyes and set the tray aside before going to join Wyss, Moreau, and now Sokolov in the cluster of sofas.

"We're calling Hansen," Fitz said. "Or we're trying to. How's it going?"

"It's this hard to call Oymyakon from here?" Moreau asked.

"It is if you're setting up a secure line," Fitz said. "Wyss?"

"Almost," Wyss said, still tapping away at the computer on his knees. Then he sat back and blew out a tired breath. Moreau picked up a half-full glass of lemon water from the table in the center of the cluster of sofas and handed it to him. He took it from her gratefully, rubbing the frosted exterior of the glass over this pale forehead before taking a sip.

"I trust you have it?" Fitz asked.

"I sent him a message," Wyss said. "I set up the secure line, but he has to initiate the call on his end. Just give him a minute."

"Well, this is probably a good time for me to tell you all something," Fitz said. He alone wasn't sitting on a sofa, and they all looked up at him expectantly. "Look, these are my personal rooms. This isn't a public space. But all that means is that the general public doesn't have access to them. Aides, cleaners, and technicians of all sorts can and do come through at their will."

"Without warning?" Sokolov asked, as if the idea offended her as a former Intergalactic Railway steward.

"Usually not, but it does happen," Fitz said. "Aside from anyone physically being in here, anyone who comes in could, of course, leave any manner of things behind."

"You mean we might be bugged?" Ritchie asked, looking around the room. Nothing looked out of place, but then it wouldn't, would it?

"Wyss did a sweep before he started the call," Fitz said. "But unless he's just done a sweep, it's best to assume that in these rooms, we will be overheard."

"Are we afraid of anyone specifically?" Ritchie started to ask, but before anyone could answer her, the wall across from Wyss lit up. What had looked like stone was now a massive screen, far larger than the one she and Fitz had once gamed on.

And it was filled with the scarred face of their mentor Colonel Ieuan Hansen, almost lost behind a curtain of static. His mouth was moving, but none of them could hear anything.

"Wyss?" Ritchie whispered.

"Give it a minute," he told her.

"Is this because it's secure?" Ritchie asked, although she wasn't sure how that would make the signal so grainy and slow.

"The delay is normal," he told her.

"I meant the image quality, but the delay is probably the bigger issue, isn't it?"

"The signal is beaming through jump space just fine," Fitz said. "It's the Oymyakon atmosphere that's futzing everything up. As usual."

Moreau started to say something but fell silent as Hansen's voice finally reached them. The face behind the static was impassive, waiting for them to respond to what they hadn't even heard yet.

"Cadets, I have to keep this short. You are all there to make contact with one of our allies. I cannot reveal their identity to you, so keep your eyes open. Do not attempt to contact me through any means besides this secure line. Even on this line I don't dare tell you any specifics about your contact. It will be up to you to find each other. Best of luck. Please confirm receipt of message."

Moreau opened her mouth to speak again, but Fitz held up a hand to belay her. Wyss leaned into his computer to say, "message received and understood."

Then the screen went blank. They could only hope that Hansen had received their response, or was still about to, or however it all worked.

"Okay, go ahead," Fitz said to Moreau, finally sinking down onto one of the sofas and reaching for his own glass of lemon water.

"We don't know who we're looking for, but they know about us, right?" she said. But there was too much uplift at the end of that question. She honestly didn't know, and neither did the rest of them.

"I certainly hope so," Ritchie said. "I don't know how this will work otherwise."

"Well, like Hansen said, we keep our eyes open," Sokolov said. "Not that I think it'll be so easy as all that. If we're looking for someone like a spy, I would certainly hope they wouldn't be identifiable as such to a bunch of cadets."

"But we're not ordinary cadets," Moreau said, tipping her glass in silent toast to Sokolov.

"Some of us are more extraordinary than others," Sokolov said, her cheeks flushing pink.

"You're worth ten ordinary cadets," Wyss told her. Flatly, as if just telling her a plain fact. They all knew Wyss didn't hand out compliments, even Sokolov, whose cheeks were red now.

"I see you're all already in formal wear for dinner," Fitz said.

"You're not," Ritchie pointed out. He was still dressed in the same uniform he had been wearing on the shuttle. For the last two days.

"Yeah, I got to grab a shower," he admitted. "Feel free to hang out here. I'll just be a minute. There's more lemon water in that pitcher on the side table."

The others all mumbled various acknowledgements as Fitz got up to head back towards his bedroom and private bathroom.

Ritchie was sorely tempted to go after him. It wasn't like she had never been in that bedroom before. And she really wanted to know what else was going on. Why had he left them right at the front door, dumping them on his staff without a word? What had he been up to since then that kept him from even getting a much-needed shower?

Something of what she was thinking must have shown on her face, because she felt Moreau's hand on her arm. Not quite restraining her, but suggesting that she stay. Ritchie gave her a questioning look, but Moreau just shook her head.

"Be patient," Moreau said. "It's only been a couple of hours."

But that just made Ritchie feel anything but patience. It was clear that Moreau knew something she didn't. And she suspected Sokolov and Wyss did as well. There were too many little looks from all of them. They kept looking at her, and looking at Fitz, like they were trying to figure out if something had happened between them.

She could even feel their disappointment that it hadn't yet. Which was just maddening.

She was giving the whole situation one evening's worth of formal dinner to resolve itself. If things didn't start making sense after that, she would jump that little wall that separated her room's balcony from Fitz's, and she would demand some answers.

She was done with always being in the dark.

4

FITZ STILL HATED the Oymyakon Foreign Service Academy's formal uniform. Every time he had to wear it, he told himself he could get through it for just one night and then he'd never have to wear it again.

But he kept having to wear it again. And again.

The design wasn't the problem, of course. All the foreign service academies used the same pants and tunic patterns. It was just the color scheme. He had been through a dozen academies in his time, and he had worn many colors proudly. Blue and silver. Green and gold. Scarlet and bronze.

But dark brown and darker brown?

Well, Fitz told himself as he and the others joined the party in progress, this time really had to be the last time. He only had one semester left, and no more breaks. This really, truly had to be the last time.

They were in the reception room outside the larger of the four dining rooms. An interior room with no windows, but projected on the ceiling overhead was a real-time image of the sky as the sunset faded to the west and stars emerged from the indigo one by one in the east.

Not that anyone there was looking up. No, they were all looking at each other. The polite ones were looking at the person in front of them or the others in their little conversation circles. The impolite ones were scanning the room for whoever it was they really wanted to talk to.

Mostly, that would be his father. But Fitz had arrived before him, apparently, as there was no sign of him anywhere in the room. He did catch his mother's eye. She smiled and waved, but the smile was an apologetic one. As much as it had been weeks since they had seen each other, she still couldn't leave the circle of people there chatting with her. But he understood. She was working. And as much as she hated being treated as a mere path to her husband, the general, she did her job well. She took that responsibility very seriously.

Fitz realized for the first time just how strange that was. He and his mother had an easy relationship. They had always just understood each other. While he and his father never understood each other and butted heads over pretty much everything. And yet his two parents were a unit, working in tandem in a way he was only now beginning to see was actually a really hard thing to pull off.

"We should split up and mingle, right?" Ritchie whispered to the other cadets.

"I agree," Moreau said. "Try to talk to as many people as you can. We'll compare notes later."

They all nodded. Wyss headed over to a cluster of various aliens all struggling to speak together in the common tongue of the Union of Free Worlds. Sokolov headed over towards Fitz's mother, although if she knew that was where she was heading, Fitz wasn't sure. The two of them had never met.

Moreau actually found another young person standing awkwardly apart from the general hubbub of the party. Dragged along by political parents, to judge by the boy's clothes. Not a military or foreign service uniform, but just as bland and clearly not his own personal choice. He was tugging at the collar of his tunic even before he saw Moreau sauntering over to him.

Ritchie didn't seem to know where she wanted to go, so she just hovered uncertainly. Fitz knew he should probably move away from her, but he had no goal in mind either.

But then he smelled something that had his mouth watering and his stomach growling. He had barely touched that noodle bowl on the shuttle. But whatever he was smelling didn't need hunger as a sauce. It was serving up the flavor all on its own.

"What is that smell? Olive oil and garlic? And what else?" Fitz mused. Not loudly, but Ritchie still spun around to hiss at him to be quieter. "What?" he asked.

"Seriously?" she said, grabbing his elbow and dragging him into an alcove. He managed to snag a tiny sandwich off a passing tray on the way, but when she spun him around to glare at him, he opted not to take a bite. "You didn't see the delgin standing right behind you, then?"

"No," Fitz said. He could feel his cheeks flushing in embarrassment. Well-deserved embarrassment. This wasn't his first formal dinner. He knew better than to say such things out loud.

But Ritchie wasn't done scowling at him. "You know, most delgins are very self-conscious about how humans perceive their pheromones as food smells."

"I know," he said. He tried raising his hands in surrender, but the sandwich still clutched in one of those hands was a distraction.

"Honestly, Fitz," she said, shaking her head even as he could tell she was fighting back a smile. "I just don't know about you sometimes."

"All I know is that the diplomat school is going to feel the loss of you," he said, taking a bite of the sandwich. It was some sort of fish paste, with sprigs of green leaves for crunch. Delicious. But then he realized she was glowering at him again. "The diplomat school's loss is the guardian's school's gain. Obviously." He took another bite of the sandwich.

Ritchie snatched the last of it from his fingers and stuffed it in her mouth, but he could see her teasing gesture give way to pleasure at the salty richness of the fish, its creamy texture perfectly encapsulated by the soft bread.

"You forgot how good our kitchen staff are," Fitz said.

But something dark passed over Ritchie's face.

"What is it?" he asked.

"Your father's here. With that other guy. Klemm," she said.

"Since Klemm joined the general's staff, the two of them have been all but joined at the hip," Fitz told her. "It's probably pointless to try now, but I *did* want to talk with my father."

He poked his head out of the alcove to find his father already in a large knot of people. Everyone wanted his attention. They always did. It really was pointless to try. There was no time for family at a party like this.

Fitz pulled his head back into the alcove to find Ritchie looking at him intently. Her face was a little too carefully expressionless. She had gotten good at that, just in the last few weeks. She never used to work so hard to hide her emotions. Not from him, anyway.

"What do you need to talk to your father about?" she asked.

Fitz sighed. "Ritchie, you know I can't tell you that."

"Not yet, is what you keep telling me," she said.

"But soon, okay?"

Her gaze, already hard, hardened further. "Not okay," she said. Then she left, disappearing among the throngs of guests.

Fitz could've happily spent the rest of the reception tucked away in that alcove, far from other people. But the food was out there, with those people.

He pushed away from the wall and found another tray of sandwiches. These were cold beef and cheese on a hard roll. Not as good as the fish ones, but he didn't really care anymore. He just wanted his stomach to quiet down.

He wandered through the crowds, avoiding the delgin just in case his faux pas *had* been overheard. He caught sight of Sokolov in the midst of an animated conversation with his mother. He wondered what they were talking about, and really hoped it wasn't him.

Moreau and the politician's son were standing together, slouched low against the wall and watching the rest of the party with visible disdain. Moreau adapting to her environment, just like she always did.

It took a little longer to find Wyss, given that the throng of aliens around him had gotten denser since the reception had started. He seemed to be tinkering with some sort of device, tech that was worn like a bracelet. Some sort of translator, perhaps? Whatever it was, the aliens gathered around him were watching him work intently.

Fitz circled around his father's crowd. He felt Klemm's eyes on him, but he didn't look over at the lieutenant. He just stopped at the next tray he reached and filled his hand with crispy egg tarts. As acts of rebellion go, it was pretty minor, but being watched clearly brought out his worst instincts.

Sadly, the egg tarts were bland. Someone at the party had a dietary preference for complete lack of seasoning, apparently, and Fitz had just rudely stocked up on their specially-made hors d'oeuvres. He had just found a table where he could dump the rest of the tarts unobserved when something caught his eye.

Ritchie, talking in a mirror?

No, Ritchie, talking to her doppelgänger. And her doppelgänger was all in white and ivory, the formal uniform of the diplomat corps. Just what she swore she would never be.

Was Fitz having some sort of waking dream experience?

He rubbed at his eyes, but both Ritchies were still there. The diplomat version had her back to him, but those honey blond curls, cut short at the level of her earlobes, were exactly the same. What was going on here?

He slipped closer to the two, trying to keep other guests between him and the Ritchie still in her Oymyakon uniform's line of sight. But the guests weren't cooperating. They kept stepping away, leaving him with the choice of either being exposed to her notice or moving further away from the two of them.

Given the hard look Ritchie had given him before, he opted to follow the cover. But the look on her face now was frightening him.

She was confused and upset. And even as he watched, he could see the needle of her emotions arc further away from confusion and deeper into upset.

There was a strange lull in the conversations around him, a dip into silence that lasted just long enough for him to hear the doppelgänger in the diplomat uniform say the word "yuffid."

He could make out no more, but he didn't need to. He needed to get to Ritchie. Now.

But by some trick of fate he couldn't remotely understand, his father got there first. Followed at once by Klemm, of course.

"Ah, Cadet Ritchie," his father said, crashing into the middle of the conversation in a way Fitz was sure he had never seen his father do before. His always-correct father had just created a huge breach in protocol. Deliberately.

"Sir," Klemm almost inaudibly said, but the general ignored him.

"Cadet Ritchie, I see you've made the acquaintance of the current special diplomat to the Buennagel governorship, Heidi Lavatar."

"Yes, she actually introduced herself to me," Ritchie said. But Fitz could tell she was still struggling with the confusion and upset from before. Now she had a third ball to juggle: behaving appropriately around senior officers.

Normally, Fitz wouldn't hesitate to bet on Ritchie. But at that particular moment, he didn't like her odds. What was his father up to?

"Ah, General Fitz, perhaps you can clear up a little misunderstanding," the diplomat Lavatar said. Her back was still to Fitz, which was maddening. Just how much like Ritchie did she look, really?

"Oh, I'm sure it's nothing," his father said. "In fact, we're about to be seated for dinner. If you'd like to get the guests moving…?"

"Of course, General," Lavatar said. "I do hope I can be seated with Cadet Ritchie, sir? I would very much like to continue our conversation."

"I'm sorry to disappoint you, Diplomat Lavatar, but I'm afraid Cadet Ritchie is to be seated next to me."

Ritchie was clearly dumbstruck, her eyes wide as she stared off into nothing. Fitz could feel his own mouth hanging open in shock and shut it before anyone else could notice him gaping.

"Sir," Ritchie managed to squeak. "I believe I'm meant to be with the other cadets. Surely?"

"You've saved my son's life," the general said.

"I think it's the other way around, sir," Ritchie said.

"On more than one occasion," he went on, as if not hearing her. "That earns you a place of honor, at my right hand."

"Sir?" Klemm said, somehow more shocked than either Ritchie or Fitz at this sudden rearrangement of seating. He had just been demoted, Fitz guessed.

"I do hope you'll find me again after dinner, Cadet Ritchie," Lavatar said, grasping Ritchie's arm as if to be sure she had her attention. "We'll go over all of it again. I don't know where we went wrong, but we'll get on the same page soon enough, I'm sure."

"I'm sure," the general said, but there was an edge of warning to his voice. Lavatar took an involuntary step back, and Fitz got his first good look at her face.

Not so much like Ritchie at all. She looked young for someone in her position, but not so young as to be mistaken for a cadet. And her brown eyes had none of Ritchie's golden flecks.

Not a doppelgänger. But a damn weird coincidence.

And now he had something *else* to ask his father about. If he ever got the opportunity.

His father, the general, took Ritchie's nerveless hand and put it over his own arm, then guided her across the reception room towards the open doors to the dining room beyond. At first, she stumbled along beside him like a sleepwalker. But then she snapped to full alertness, her head swiveling as her eyes scanned the room she was all too quickly departing.

She caught Fitz's eye at last, her own eyes filled with panic. He took half a step towards them, but then his father turned his head to give him a reproachful look.

Somehow, Fitz got the sense that he wasn't going to be seated anywhere near the head of the table. Which left Ritchie all on her own, at the mercy of his father.

The father who still hadn't spoken with him. It was all so maddening. Fitz, grinding his teeth, fell into step with the others making their way into the dining room.

The only small consolation was the bereft look on Lieutenant Klemm's face as he stood rooted in place, just where the general had abandoned him, in the middle of the emptying reception room.

5

RITCHIE KNEW they were on a mission. She knew she had a job to do. But dinner had been such a confusing and emotionally traumatic affair, she had slipped away even before dessert was served. A trip to the bathroom became a run up the stairs to her room on the fourteenth floor.

Now she stood alone on her balcony looking up at all the stars, and watching how the wind made the grass below flash with silvery light, reflecting the two moons above. It was a warm night, and the crickets were singing so loudly she could hear them all the way up to where she was.

She didn't regret her decision to flee at all. She had seen the fancy desserts being arranged on carts as she had left the dining room. Something decadently creamy and chocolatey that had a texture like pudding but was formed into squares like cake. She didn't regret not having any. Despite being too far away to smell the Immerweis, her mind was still achingly nostalgic for the candy.

But she wasn't sure she wanted any of that either. Not unless she could make a batch with her mother, like she had as a little girl. And that, of course, was impossible.

There was a rustle from the balcony beside her. At first she thought it was just the wind twisting at the gauzy drapes, but then the drapes parted and a figure emerged to join her at the railing to overlook the prairie.

It was Fitz.

"Did you come to bring me back?" Ritchie asked. She didn't regret leaving the party, but if he reminded her of their mission, she'd have to give in. She'd have to go back and finish the job. And somehow find a way to avoid his father and his father's new diplomat both.

"No," Fitz said, still leaning on his elbows and looking out over the night.

"Just wanted a breath of fresh air?" Ritchie asked. "Surely the patio off the library was closer."

"It was," Fitz said. Then he finally looked over at her. Not that she could tell more than that the outline of his head changed shape when he turned it toward her. The moonlight that lit up the grasslands was somehow much dimmer up on the balcony. "I wanted to see if you wanted to talk about it?"

"Talk about what?" Ritchie asked, but her heart was already beating faster. He knew already, didn't he? He knew what that woman had said to her. Heidi Lavatar.

"Whatever it is that made you run away," he said. "That's not like you, Ritchie. It's pretty worrying for the rest of us."

"So the others sent you as spokesperson?" she asked.

"Of course I had to come. It's my father that upset you, isn't it?"

"No," she said. "Well, not at first."

"You seemed shocked by whatever Diplomat Lavatar said to you, but the running away came after four courses at my father's right hand, not after what she said. Am I wrong?"

"No, you're not wrong," she said. "I don't even understand why I was put there, with no warning at all. It must've been a last-minute change, to judge from how put out that Klemm fellow was."

"It was at the latest of all possible minutes," Fitz said. Then he took a deep breath, as if bracing himself for whatever he was about to say next. "It was because of what Diplomat Lavatar said. I heard only a little, but I know he heard more. And he made sure that the conversation was over. That's why he changed the seating chart. I'm not sure what he had planned for after dinner, but I guess you just solved that problem for him."

"He was doing me a kindness?" Ritchie said with very heavy skepticism.

"Maybe. Probably not," Fitz said. His attention was back out of the grasslands again. She could feel it happening, that withdrawing thing he did when he didn't want to talk to her about something. Something specific.

"I didn't need to be rescued from her at all, you know," Ritchie said. "She wasn't being cruel or anything. She seems very competent at her job, despite her young age. In fact, she initially approached me because she wanted to offer to mentor me. Like so many others, she was under the misapprehension that I wanted to be a diplomat."

"You can't blame people for seeing that you would be uniquely good at it," Fitz said.

"It's not my calling," Ritchie said.

"So you told her no?" he asked.

"I told her I was going to guardian school, yes," Ritchie said. "And she was flabbergasted. I don't think I've ever used that word before, but it totally fits."

"Like she was offended?" Fitz asked.

"No, just shocked and surprised. You know, flabbergasted."

It was a real possibility that Fitz had never heard the word before. But he just nodded. Which could mean anything, really.

"I hope I didn't blow it. What if she is the contact we are here to meet?" Ritchie said. She said it out loud first, but the thought of it clicked in her mind and then just exploded. "Fitz, what if she was our contact? I mean, she was specifically talking about meeting with me on Braga while I'm a student there. Of advising me and guiding my academic career. Doesn't that sound like what we're looking for here?"

"I think what we're looking for here is going to be a little harder to see at first," Fitz said. "Spy craft, you know."

"I don't know," Ritchie said, feeling even more miserable than when she had fled up to her room. "I think I really blew it."

"I don't think you did," Fitz said. Then he made a little frustrated sound before vaulting over the low wall that divided their two balconies. Now she could see his face, although his eyes were still opaque to her.

"How could you know that? You weren't even there," she said.

"I was close enough to hear how the conversation ended," he said.

"Your father ended it," Ritchie pointed out.

"Yes, but she still wanted to talk to you. In fact, I'm sure she's downstairs right now, grilling Moreau and Sokolov and Wyss, asking where you are. I'm sure she still wants to talk to you. She's not our contact; I think I'm pretty positive about that. But even if she were, you didn't burn that bridge. Okay?"

Now it was Ritchie turning away to look out over the prairie. But only partly to avoid meeting those inscrutable eyes. Mostly it was because the moonlight dancing along the blades of grass and the leaves of the flowers really was soothing.

But not so soothing that her mind wasn't still preoccupied with what had been said before dinner.

"What *did* you hear?" Ritchie asked. She had no idea why she was speaking so softly, like she was afraid of being overheard. But Fitz stepped closer to lean against the balcony beside her, their elbows resting on the top of the ledge touching.

"Something about the yuffids," he said. "Did she bring up your father? I suppose she must have. She holds his position now. There was only one other diplomat who served between them."

"No," Ritchie said, half-closing her eyes as she brought all the words of the conversation back to mind. "Now that you mention it, it was like she avoided speaking of him as much as it was possible. She just kept talking about 'the diplomatic mission.' But no one was on that mission except for my father."

"What did she say, then?" Fitz asked.

"She said..." Ritchie began, but it was like all the gears in her brain just crashed all at once. She was surprised that Fitz couldn't hear the metallic shriek before it all ground to a halt. She had no words.

But she still had questions.

"Ritchie?"

"I need to see the video from the day my father was taken," Ritchie said, her hands twisting together. "Can you believe I've never watched it? Not even once?"

"I can believe it," Fitz said. "If it were my father, I don't think I would."

"Yes, you would," Ritchie said, without hesitation. "You would face it."

"When I was twelve, I wouldn't have," Fitz said. "And with every day that passes, it becomes more and more pointless to see it, doesn't it? It doesn't change anything."

"It feels a lot less pointless today," Ritchie said.

"What did she say to you?" he asked again.

But still, she didn't want to answer. Instead, she asked him, "you've seen it, haven't you?"

"I saw it live," Fitz said. Those words hit her like a blow, and she involuntarily sucked in a breath. But he kept talking. "In my father's office. And I've seen it a few times since."

"And you never told me?" she demanded. But her anger wasn't there for her, as much as she wanted it to cloak her in its protective fire. No, all she had was shock and hurt.

"You left so fast," he said. Lamely, to her ears.

"But you saw," Ritchie said. She shoved his shoulder, forcing him to turn towards her so she could jab him hard right in the solar plexus. He let out a woof of air and took half a step back. "You *saw*?"

"She told you about the gesture," Fitz said, and it took Ritchie a minute to work out that he was still talking about Diplomat Lavatar.

"Of course that's what she told me," Ritchie said, blinking back hot tears. "She..." Her breath caught, like she had a wicked stitch in her side from running, and it took a minute to get her wind back enough to gasp on. "She wrote a paper about it. In diplomat school. It was her senior project. The importance of nonverbal communication in alien species, with a particular focus on my father's encounter with the yuffids."

Her words came out brittle and sharp, and even in the darkness she could see Fitz wince at every one. But it wasn't enough.

"You knew, and you never told me," Ritchie said. "And I just don't get it. Why?"

Fitz had his hands half-raised, like he was afraid she would hit him again. And if she were angry, she might try to. But she wasn't angry. Her breath was coming in painful hitches because she couldn't stop sobbing.

"Come here," Fitz said, catching her wrist and drawing her towards him. She bristled, thinking he was going to try hugging her—as if that were remotely what she needed just then. But he was just trying to move her a little further away from the edge. From the fourteen-floor drop.

"Why didn't you tell me?" she demanded.

"Ritchie, isn't it obvious?" he asked, still pulling her after him until they reached a bench built into the wall between the doors to her room and the low wall separating her balcony from the next.

"I so don't need you making me feel stupid right now," she growled at him.

"I'm not doing that. I swear," Fitz said. He guided her down onto the bench, then sat beside her, turned to face her. But she refused to look at him. She focused instead on the two moons. One was silver, but the other was golden. How had she forgotten that?

"I saw what happened live in my father's office," Fitz reminded her. "I saw it with my father. We were the only two to see it live. And he swore I was never to tell a soul what I saw there on that screen. Not even you. Especially not you."

"Why?" Ritchie demanded.

"I think at first he hoped he could suppress it. But, of course, that was impossible. Your father was too important a diplomat for his disappearance to go unremarked. You and your mother were moved at once. For your own safety, he told me."

"Was he lying about everything? Why?" Ritchie asked.

"I honestly don't know," Fitz said. He dropped his head into his hands and tore at his hair. "I came here for one reason only. To ask my father about all of that. I wanted to have the answers before I told you. Because I know there's more going on than I know, but I do know you're in danger. Now that you know, you're in danger."

"What do I know that everyone else doesn't know?" Ritchie asked.

"Diplomat Lavatar wrote a paper on the topic. All of it is public knowledge. What is the secret?"

"You are, Ritchie," he said. Which made no sense. "Look, I'm guessing Diplomat Lavatar didn't get a chance to tell you about her paper in detail?"

"No. I assume because she was being polite and not telling me how my father failed so epically." Then she was crying again. "He failed because he took my advice. Nothing I ever do is going to make up for that. And don't tell me it's okay because I was just a kid. Don't even say it!"

"I wasn't going to," Fitz said.

There it was again, that little expectant pause, like he was about to say more. And then he didn't.

"Just say it, Fitz," Ritchie said. "For the love of everything, just spit it out already."

She expected him to agree that she had messed up. But that would surely be followed by another pointless pep talk. To bolster her spirits. She was pretty sure she could still push him over the balcony from here if he tried.

But what he said was, "you didn't fail him, Ritchie. My father did."

"What?" Ritchie asked. She knew that word came out all hateful and angry, but she was pretty sure he was making a joke, and this really wasn't the time.

"You were right about the gesture," he said. "I told my father. I don't know what happened then. Maybe the message didn't get through? Maybe he chose not to send it because he didn't think much of a twelve-year-old's language skills? Or—and this is the alternative that has kept me up so very many nights—maybe he didn't pass it on on purpose."

"Why?" Ritchie asked, barely more than a whisper.

"That's what I came here to ask him," Fitz said. Then he scoffed at himself. "I was going to talk to him and then you, but that wasn't working out. And I couldn't go any longer without telling you."

"But wait," Ritchie said, still confused. "What is Lavatar's paper about then? If my father never did the gesture?"

"Someone else worked out what you did, some years later," Fitz told her. "It's been talked about since. But no one alive knows you came up with it first. So as much as you want to fume about everyone admiring your potential as a diplomat, the real irony is no one knows your real big break-through. My father has very handily suppressed all knowledge of that."

"That's why my mother and I moved so quickly?" Ritchie asked.

"I think so," Fitz said. "And I'm sorry, but it's also why he worked so hard to keep you out of all the foreign service academies. Wyss can prove it to you if you doubt me."

"Why would I doubt you?" Ritchie asked.

"Why would you *trust* me?" Fitz shot back. Then his head was in his hands again, fingers twisting and pulling at his hair. It had to be painful.

She reached out to touch him, but her hand hovered over his shaking shoulder before dropping back to her own lap. Why should she comfort him now? He could've told her all this years ago. He could've spared them both so much pain.

"Why indeed?" she murmured, mostly to herself, but partly to him. "Finn Berweger knows, right? And Moreau and Sokolov and Wyss? What about Hansen?" He didn't answer, but now that she was casting her mind back, a lot of things were starting to look suspiciously like *everyone* but her had known. "Cadmar Weld? Sidonie Keller?"

"They were guessing," Fitz said, his voice muffled through his hands.

"They were better guessers than me, then," Ritchie said. She got up from the bench. "You can go back the way you came, right?" But she didn't wait for an answer. She just went into the guest room and closed all the doors to the balcony, bolting every lock and closing every curtain.

Then she laid down on her bed and didn't sleep at all.

6

FITZ SPENT A LONG, sleepless night staring at the ceiling of his bedroom and wishing he would've said everything differently the night before.

Which didn't take away from his relief that it was finally over. But he was pretty sure he had bungled it.

Finally, he couldn't stand lying there arguing with himself for a minute more. He got up, pulled on the tunic and shirt that on Oymyakon served as his physical training uniform, then headed barefoot out to his sitting room. He knew that despite dawn barely brightening the sky to the east, someone from the kitchens had already been upstairs to lie out a breakfast buffet. He could smell the coffee and toast.

Not that he was remotely hungry. The idea of food had little appeal to him, despite the delicious smell of melted butter. He just needed that coffee to get the sticky morning taste out of his mouth as much as to zap him to a semblance of a state of wakefulness he was going to have to fake all day.

It was going to be a very long day.

The stone tile was smooth and warm under his feet, and the birds outside the window were singing their happiness about the sunrise. It couldn't be more the opposite of waking up back at school. But it couldn't penetrate the fog of his mind enough to cheer him.

He stumbled into the sitting room, looking around for the food he could smell. He found it, set out on a sideboard that stood against one of the central pillars of the ridiculously large room. The immense samovar containing the coffee was shining brightly silver, reflecting the first rays of the dawning sun.

He was halfway to it before he realized he was not alone. Wyss was already there, sitting on one of the sofas with his knees drawn up to his chin, eyes locked on a tablet. And so were Moreau and Sokolov, sitting together at a little table that had definitely not been there the night before. It was the sort of table that would be inside a cafe, just room enough for two. And there were two more just like it on either side of them.

They all looked up as he shuffled into the room, and he realized he was the only one not in uniform.

"A bit early, isn't it?" Fitz asked as he continued on to the samovar and filled a mug with dark coffee.

"Is it?" Moreau asked him.

He lifted the mug to his lips, but before he had taken a sip, the door directly in his line of sight opened and Ritchie came into the room. She saw him looking straight at her and flushed, then scurried over to Moreau and Sokolov. Like the others, she was already dressed in her cadet uniform with her hair correctly arranged. But her eyes were red from too much crying and too little sleep.

Fitz was instantly glad he hadn't yet had a chance to complain about his bad night.

He almost took a sip again, but before he could, Moreau was there, gesturing for him to move out of her way. He stepped aside, then watched as she assembled a cup of very sweet black tea and a plate of buttered toast. She then carried those, as well as a little pot of some sort of red-colored jam, back to her table.

For Ritchie.

He wondered if Ritchie had already told Moreau everything. They were buddies. They slept in the same room. She must have.

"Fitz," Wyss said, waving a hand to catch his attention. Fitz moved around to the back of the sofa so he could see what was on Wyss screen, but before any of it quite came into focus, his mother was bursting into the room.

"Mom?" Fitz asked, quickly setting the mug of hot coffee aside before running to catch hold of her. He had never seen her so distraught.

"You're all here? You're all well?" she asked, looking around the room even as she squeezed Fitz's arms, as if needing to assure herself that he was real.

"We're all here and we're fine," he said. "What's going on?"

"There was a murder," Wyss said. "I just saw it come up on the news feed."

"Already?" Fitz's mother said weakly. She pressed a trembling hand to her forehead for a moment. Then she straightened, all emotion set aside as she calmly took charge. "I was hoping for a little more time before all hell breaks loose, but so be it. I just needed to check on you all first."

"Wait, Mom," Fitz said, catching her arm before she could dart back out the door. "What happened?"

"Just as Wyss told you. There's been a murder," she said, and tried to yank her arm out of his grasp. But he held firm.

"Who? Where?" he asked.

"It was our new diplomat. Heidi Lavatar. In her home," she told him.

He had a thousand more questions. And he was all too aware of how intently Ritchie was watching them both, hand to her mouth in shock even before Lavatar's name was mentioned. And he remembered that of course the scene of the murder, the diplomat's house, was her childhood home.

Like she needed more emotional trauma heaped on top of everything that had gone down the night before.

"I'm sorry, Fitz. I'll tell you more when I know more, but just now —" his mother started to say. But she broke off, turning as the door behind her banged open and two guardians came into the room. They worked for Buennagel security, to judge by their uniforms, but neither were among the officers Fitz had met the day before.

"Don't you knock?" Fitz demanded. The dark-skinned man whose name tag read WAHLI flushed but said nothing. The pale woman whose tag said RODIN just scowled at him.

"Hush, Fitz," his mother said, then gave him a little shove. "Please, go sit with your friends."

Fitz let her push him away. He dropped down beside Wyss, who tilted his tablet in a way that clearly indicated he wanted Fitz to look at it. The two guardians were whispering with his mother, and she was whispering back, but he had no clue what words were passing between them.

"What's this?" Fitz asked, tipping the tablet further so he could get a better look at the screen.

"No witnesses," Wyss told him in a low voice. "The security system was disabled. By someone who knew what they were doing."

"You've hacked into my family's security system?" Fitz asked him.

"I did that back on Jorda. The same codes got me in here," Wyss said. "Shocking, really. I have to bring that up with your father."

"Yeah, you do that," Fitz said. He couldn't imagine having that conversation with his father himself.

"Cadets," his mother said, clasping her hands together as they all looked her way expectantly. "I'm sorry this unfortunate turn of events is putting a damper on your time here."

"We're used to murder disrupting things," Fitz said. His mother shot him a look that let him know she didn't find that comment funny.

"Have you found the murder weapon?" Wyss asked. Fitz tried to sneak another look at the tablet. The official word must still be no weapon found or else Wyss wouldn't ask.

But neither of the guardians said a word. They just stood there, waiting with their hands folded behind their backs.

"That's not something they can reveal yet," Fitz's mother said. "Don't worry, I'm sure this will all be cleared up as soon as possible. The guardians who work here are practiced in investigations. In addition to securing this building, they oversee all the departments all over the planet. It's all in good hands."

Fitz had no idea who she was hoping to soothe. He and Ritchie might have been kids when they lived here, but they well knew how those things worked. Moreau, Sokolov and Wyss might not know specifically how the security forces on Buennagel were structured, but they could glean enough from the insignias on the guardians' uniforms.

"But?" Fitz said, because there had to be something she was dancing around. Aside from the fact she was stating the obvious, she would be gone already, dealing with the more politically important guests, if there wasn't something more.

The guests far more likely than the five of them to fear being targets themselves.

"These guardians would like a word with Cadet Ritchie," Fitz's mother said, then hold out her hand for Ritchie to join her.

"Why don't they just talk to her here? There are no secrets between us," Fitz said.

Ritchie shot him an incredulous but also furious look, and he sunk lower into the sofa, certain his ears were hotly red.

That had definitely been the wrong thing to say.

"You *can* speak to me here," Ritchie said, as she stopped in front of the two guardians, ignoring his mother's imploring hand. "I'm happy to answer any questions. I have nothing to hide."

Fitz chewed at his lip, fighting the urge to throw himself physically into the mix, to intervene before… what?

What could they possibly have to ask her? Everyone had seen his father interrupt Ritchie's conversation with the diplomat-now-murder-victim Lavatar, but so what? It hadn't been anything remotely like a heated argument. There was no way she could be considered a suspect.

Was there?

"Do you recognize this weapon?" Guardian Wahli asked and handed Ritchie a tablet. She took it from him and used her fingers to rotate and expand the image.

"I'm not sure," she said. Then she rotated the image again and sucked in a breath. "Yes, actually. I do. It's hanging on the wall in the guest room I'm staying in."

"Are you sure? It's there now?" Guardian Rodin asked. A little too eagerly for Fitz's tastes. Like she had just caught Ritchie in a lie.

"No, I'm not sure," Ritchie said. "I've been here for the last ten minutes or so."

"But it was there on the wall when you left?" Rodin pressed.

Ritchie rotated the image again. "I don't know. I wasn't paying attention."

"Was it there last night when you went to bed?" Wahli asked.

"I definitely wasn't paying attention then," Ritchie said. "I'm sorry. I just don't know. Do you want to go look now?"

"No need," he said, and took the tablet back from her.

"That was the murder weapon?" Fitz asked. Ritchie shot him a look over her shoulder, warning him not to interfere before returning her attention to the security officers.

"If it was removed from the wall, I really don't know when that happened," Ritchie said. "If it's even the knife I'm thinking of, I don't remember seeing it or not seeing it since long before dinner last night. Everything after that was... a little overwhelming. I'm sorry, but I really wasn't paying attention to the room decorations after that."

"So there'd be no reason for your DNA to be anywhere on this weapon?" Wahli asked.

Ritchie started to shake her head no, but then she stopped, pressing a knuckle to her mouth as she pondered.

"Cadet?" Rodin prompted.

"I think I might have touched it," Ritchie said. "Just a little, when I was looking at it yesterday afternoon."

"You touched it?" Rodin asked.

"Just a fingertip, like this," Ritchie said, raising a single finger and miming touching something, lifting it a little, then letting it drop. "I didn't close my hand around it or anything. And I know you can tell the difference."

"You are correct," Wahli said, tapping the tablet against his open palm. "We will be able to tell. As soon as we get the results back."

"Okay. So that's all right, then," Ritchie said, but Fitz could see her shifting her weight from foot to foot nervously.

"There's no need to fret," Rodin said with a tight smile. "Of course we believe you. But we'll probably have more questions for you later. After the results come back."

"I'll be here," Ritchie said.

The two guardians looked at each other, then filed out of the room. Fitz's mother gave Ritchie a quick hug and whispered something in her ear before departing after them.

"There's always a murder," Wyss said drily, his eyes locked onto his tablet once more.

Fitz looked at Ritchie standing there facing the closed door, her hands curled into tense fists. He wanted to do something, to say something to her. But he was pretty sure if he tried, he would only make things worse.

Why did so much have to pile up all at once? His father, her father, and now a murder? And despite their words, those officers had been giving Ritchie pretty strong "potential suspect" lookovers.

"Come on, Ritchie," Moreau said. "Tea and toast. Once that's gone, we'll figure out the next step. We always do."

"I'm in the security systems," Wyss said to the room at large. "I'll know what they know, when they know it. We'll stay on top of this thing."

"Right," Ritchie said, and sat down between Moreau and Sokolov. She let one of them shove tea at her, the other the plate of toast, but she didn't touch either. "The first step is figuring out who the suspects are. It's going to be tricky this time. We don't know anyone here, but this place and that party were thick with political intrigue."

"We're going to need an entire wall to lay out a diagram," Moreau said, and pushed the tea closer to her.

"We can start with just a list," Ritchie said. Then she took a drink from that tea, almost as if she didn't realize she was doing it. Her thoughts were all on solving the murder.

"There were some diplomats there who were jealous that she got so elevated a job at such a young age," Sokolov said. "We can start there."

"Then there are political enemies of Buennagel, since she's the diplomat in residence here," Moreau said.

Ritchie nodded, chewing on a corner of toast as she watched Sokolov writing out names that Fitz couldn't see.

Not that he needed to. They all had this well in hand without him.

He went back to the samovar for another cup of coffee. But his thoughts weren't really on the murder. They were on his father.

Where was he now? And how much harder was it going to be to get a moment alone with him, with a murder investigation going on all around them?

The timing really sucked.

7

IT MIGHT HAVE BEEN MORE annoying, the way Moreau and Sokolov both were constantly trying to get more breakfast in her, if the food hadn't been so good. The coffee had nothing in it, no sugar or syrups or even cream, but the rich roasted flavor needed no such adornment. And the caffeine hit her with surgical precision, clearing the sleep from her tired brain without making her hands shake or her teeth chatter.

And plain toast with butter had no reason to be such a distraction. But it had been a long time since she'd had butter made from cows she could walk over and visit if she wanted to. The freshness made a difference. It was almost as if she could taste the grasses and flowers of her home world there in that creamy yellow butter. And it melted into all the nooks of the sourdough bread without soaking through to get on her fingers.

But when Sokolov brought a third plate of toast to the little table where she was working, it really was too much.

"Guys, I promise you, I'm okay," she said, catching Moreau's sleeve to keep her from fetching more coffee. "Really."

"Well, it's not like you've not been accused of murder before," Moreau agreed.

"But you were upset before that," Sokolov said. "You don't look like you slept at all last night. That couldn't be because of what happened to the diplomat."

"No, that was something else," Ritchie said. She could see Sokolov had followup questions, so she opted to steer the conversation in another direction. "Listen, I'm sure we're all thinking it, but I'm going to say it out loud, anyway."

"You think you know who did this? Already?" Moreau asked, trying to sneak a peek at the list Ritchie had been scrawling on her tablet.

"Well, isn't it obvious?" Ritchie asked. They all just blinked at her, and a little knot of worry twisted in her stomach. She hadn't slept. Her emotions were still in a turmoil she was just barely keeping under the surface. Maybe she was off her game?

"Tell us," Fitz said, from so far on the other end of the room he was in shadow even now that the midmorning sun was nearly level with the eastern windows.

"I think it was the general," Ritchie said. She could feel her cheeks flushing hotly, but she pressed on. "He was the most upset about what the diplomat had been saying. Maybe he had warned her ahead of time not to say a word. Maybe she'd broken an order when she spoke to me."

"About what?" Sokolov asked.

Ritchie considered her answer carefully. "It wasn't a state secret. Not exactly. But it was something the general is apparently very interested in keeping secret. Him, and only him. I don't know. To me, it makes sense."

Moreau and Sokolov exchanged a glance. Ritchie could feel how on edge they both were. They shared questions about what Ritchie had just said, but they also shared a concern about how to phrase them. They didn't know what she knew. They didn't know how to ask without letting something slip. They almost had her pity.

But in the end, they both just fixed their gazes back on their own crumb-strewn plates and said nothing.

"Fitz? What do you think?" Wyss asked.

Fitz strolled back into the morning light, but only to go back to the samovar for yet another refill of his coffee. He blew the steam from the surface of the mug before answering. "I don't agree. I don't think my father is a murderer. He's certainly not this murderer."

"If the diplomat was killed for what she told you, do you think you might be next? Whoever the murderer is?" Sokolov asked.

Ritchie bit at her lip. She hadn't even considered that possibility. But, like being accused of murder, being a potential victim wasn't exactly new to her.

"All I know is the general kept her from talking," she said. "And he made sure I sat beside him all through dinner so he could hear everything else that was said to me. Which was nothing he didn't say himself. No one else dared speak to me."

"What did he say to you?" Moreau asked. "Anything that might be a clue?"

"Not really," Ritchie said. "He only said what he was required to. 'Here's the soup. Pass the salt.' That sort of thing. But he never stopped glaring at me. Not even for a second."

"He was giving you a lot of dark looks back at the shuttle platform on Oymyakon when he picked us up." Moreau said, and Sokolov nodded her agreement. "Not that he was warm with any of us. Well, except Wyss."

"He likes me," Wyss said with a shrug.

"Or he thinks you might be useful to him someday," Moreau said.

"That's as close as my father gets to liking anyone," Fitz said. "Look, he's a grump. He likes to barge through life like a constant storm cloud, always on the verge of ruining everyone's day. And if you cross him, definitely look out. But again, I don't see him killing a diplomat that works for him. And I definitely don't see him breaking into Ritchie's room to steal a knife from the wall to frame her for the murder."

"I would think framing her fits his profile even more than killing the diplomat," Moreau said. "We all know he worked very hard to tank her academic career already."

An awkward silence fell over the room. Ritchie, who had been munching on another slice of toast that she absolutely didn't need, took a moment before she realized that Moreau's face was scarlet.

"Oh, I know about that," Ritchie said, speaking with her mouth full, but the moment seemed to demand an immediate answer.

"You… know about that?" Moreau stammered.

"I know all of it," Ritchie said, setting aside the rest of her toast and wiping the crumbs from her fingers.

Everyone looked to Fitz.

"Yeah. She knows," he said. His voice sounded half-strangled, like it was a struggle to get the words out.

"Everything?" Sokolov asked, looking from Ritchie and Fitz, then back again.

"She knows everything I know," Fitz said.

"Well, finally!" Moreau said with immense relief. She reached for both of Ritchie's hands and gave them a tight squeeze. "That explains why you were up all night."

"I'm sorry we knew before you," Sokolov said with genuine feeling. But then a look of confusion fell over her face. "Wait, what does this mean? Aren't you in danger now? Oh no! Is that what this is? Because you know?"

"It's a theory," Ritchie said.

"No, it's not," Fitz said firmly. "My father didn't do this."

"Okay, let's set him aside as a suspect," Moreau said, still squeezing Ritchie's hands. "Whoever *did* do this, isn't that a possible motive? Someone knows Ritchie knows?"

"Why would anyone kill Diplomat Lavatar because Fitz finally told me the truth?" Ritchie asked.

"I don't know. Maybe it's a longshot," Moreau said. "But she was killed in what used to be your house. And I can't be the only one who noticed she looks an awful lot like you."

"She does," Sokolov and Wyss said together.

"Especially from behind, and at a distance," Fitz agreed.

"Does she?" Ritchie said. She had been so distracted by the words coming out of Heidi Lavatar's mouth, she hadn't really taken in more of her appearance than the newness of her uniform.

"She does," Moreau said. "Is that a theory?"

"No one knows I told Ritchie anything except you all, just now,"

Fitz said. "I used Wyss' little toy to check the balcony for bugs before I even went out there."

"You did?" Ritchie said, surprised she hadn't noticed that. But then again, she had been pretty focused on her own inner turmoil.

"I did, and Wyss did again this morning, right?" Fitz asked.

Wyss nodded. "I was the first one in here, so I decided to use my time wisely."

"Oh, I've just had another terrible idea," Sokolov said, pressing her hands to her pale cheeks. "What if the diplomat was our contact?"

"Fitz is sure she isn't," Ritchie said. Then winced. "Or wasn't."

"Then why didn't anyone get in contact with any of us?" Sokolov asked.

"Didn't they? We haven't compared notes on the dinner party yet," Moreau said, looking around at the others.

"I talked to as many people as I could, but no one seemed to be giving me any kind of signal," Sokolov said.

"I spoke to every alien being at least once. Ditto," Wyss said.

"I saw nothing," Fitz said.

"But you left early," Moreau said, and gave Ritchie half a glance. "Actually, you both did. Maybe that's our answer. Whoever is here to meet us decided the moment wasn't right. Because we weren't all there. Or maybe they wanted to make contact with one of the two of you first."

"It's a possibility," Fitz said with a shrug. But to Ritchie's ears, he didn't sound like he believed that at all.

"Maybe our contact is someone we'll meet today or tomorrow. Maybe they aren't here yet," she said.

"So we just continue keeping an eye out, then," Sokolov said.

"While we solve this murder," Moreau said, tapping Ritchie's tablet as if it somehow already held all the answers. "But can I just say what a relief it is that everything is finally out in the open? I hated keeping secrets from you, buddy. But especially that one. It was so huge."

Ritchie nodded, not trusting herself to form words.

"We all hated it," Sokolov said. Now it was her turn to catch Ritchie's hands in a reassuring squeeze.

"If this murder isn't about Ritchie, she still might be a target for an attack from a different source, right?" Wyss asked.

"That's my fear," Fitz said. His gaze was fixed down at his own bare feet on the stone tile, not willing to meet anyone's eyes, Ritchie could tell. She knew his body language so well.

"The Berwegers aren't here," Ritchie said softly. "That at least makes me feel safer. Even if that feeling of safety is irrational. An illusion."

"We all feel better when they're not around," Moreau said.

"It's not the twins I fear so much as their parents," Fitz said. "They've been a huge threat, and they've never even met Ritchie or been on the same planet as her, ever. They work behind the scenes, using proxies. Which means they could be anywhere. Anyone around us could be working for them, and we won't know until it's too late."

"Do you think your father is in league with them?" Wyss asked.

Fitz just stared down at his feet without answering. Finally, he mumbled, "I still really need to speak with my father. I'll just have to lead with telling him that I've told you everything. I guarantee he's going to want a word with me after he knows that."

Another awkward silence fell over the room.

Then Sokolov tried to muster up a smile and said, "still, this is like old times, right? All of us on the same page, solving a crime together? Just like we used to."

"It does feel more like it used to," Moreau agreed.

Wyss was too deep in his tablet to be following the conversation around him anymore. Which sort of back up Sokolov's point. But she and Moreau were both looking at Ritchie, waiting eagerly for her to agree too.

Only Ritchie couldn't. She just couldn't.

"Sorry, not to me," she said. Her words came out more bitter than she intended, but she knew the two of them would understand. They knew who the bitterness was really for. The boy still starting at his own feet. "Nothing can be like the good old days for me. Because the good old days were all about me being in the dark about the most significant event of my entire life. I don't ever want to go back there."

"We understand," Moreau said softly.

"Do you?" Ritchie asked. "Because for me, there are no good old days. Not unless you go all the way back to before my father was taken from me. And I still don't know why that happened."

Moreau and Sokolov both stared silently down at their plates. But her words weren't really meant for them, anyway.

When the silence stretched on too maddeningly long, Ritchie looked up to see whether Fitz had fallen into a catatonic state or what. Why wasn't he answering?

He wasn't answering because he was gone. Without a word, he had just slipped away.

Ritchie bit painfully down on her lip, beyond frustrated. The one thing she had hoped would change—his constant avoidance of talking to her—was still there. As strong as ever.

And what could she possibly do to change that?

8

AS FITZ STOOD in the middle of his father's darkened, empty office, he realized he had never been inside it when his father wasn't there before. Ever. He looked back at the door behind him, belatedly wondering why the security system had let him inside. He must have permission. And if he had permission, that had to have come from his father?

But what could that possibly mean? His father didn't trust him. At all.

At least he knew for sure now that the fact this room made him feel small and cold wasn't a side effect of his towering, hot-headed father always being there. The absence of his father was felt, certainly. But the stone bookcases still towered over Fitz. The stone tiles under his bare feet were almost frigidly cold, a marked contrast to the warm tiles of his own rooms or the thick carpet of the corridors he had traversed to get here. He sat down in the leather chair before the stone desk, partly to get his feet off that floor but partly to test how it felt.

Yep. He still felt like a little kid drowning in the padded leather.

Fitz decided to just give in to that feeling, drawing up his feet and curling up into the depths of the chair, chewing at a thumbnail.

What if Ritchie was right? What if his father was trying to kill her? What if he had killed the diplomat already?

No, he just didn't believe that was true. There were all sorts of things he wouldn't put past his father, including even possibly murder, if the circumstances required it. But not this murder. It just didn't feel like any of it had his father's signature to it.

He looked over at his father's desk, currently inert. That was definitely security-locked against him. Wyss could possibly break into it, given enough time alone with it. Fitz stood no chance, even given infinite time, which he definitely didn't have. No reason to even try touching it, then.

Not that he was afraid of getting caught. Nosing through his father's things was a far lesser crime than the one he was desperately trying to confess to, if he could just find his father.

A sudden sneeze took him, then a second and a third. It wasn't from the cold, or from any kind of dust or ash in the air. Dust never had a chance to settle here; the housekeeping robots were too over-programmed for that to happen. And the massive fireplace was probably the coldest point in the room. It might have been used, back when his grandfather was still governor, but never once since his father took over.

Another sneeze had him fleeing from the room. It was pointless to wait for his father there, anyway. And he was pretty sure what was making him sneeze was all those books. Even lovingly preserved, paper pages were just not something he was used to breathing. The musty smell of them all was coating the back of his tongue in a way even yet another trio of sneezes didn't clear.

He needed something to get the taste out of his mouth. He headed towards the kitchens, but guardian investigators combing over the formal dining room and its reception hall forced him to take a more circuitous route to the back of the house.

What were they hoping to find? He supposed they were just being thorough. But if they did find anything at all, Wyss would know about it. No reason for Fitz to linger and watch them search.

The kitchens were the exact opposite of his father's office in every aspect except their size. They extended from one end of the building to the other, across the entire back end of the second floor. So there were windows on three sides, and they were all opened to the sunlight and the smell of the grass and the songs of the birds. The breeze warmed the air, and the ovens that never stopped baking bread day or night were warmer still.

They were also full of people working singly or in quietly chatting groups. The warmth and the occasional bursts of laughter as cooks darted around each other with practiced ease made the whole room feel snug and cozy. But hundreds of people would eat well by what these kitchens produced on a daily basis.

Fitz had come in search of water, but a handful of tart miniature tomatoes found their way into his mouth first. They were still sun-warm from the gardens and burst between his teeth in spurts of juice.

"Fitz! Still in your pajamas!" his mother cried as she crossed the room to where he was filling a glass with water. She spun and darted around the constantly-in-motion cooks with the practiced ease of a dancer.

"I was looking for father," he said.

"Oh, Fitz. It's just as well you haven't found him yet. You know you should really be dressed before you do," she chided him.

"When he hears what I have to say, it's not going to matter," Fitz said.

"Do you have to do this now?" she asked him. "There's nothing you can do to help with this investigation. I know you and your friends have earned a reputation for doing just that, but please don't. Not this time. Not with your father."

"It actually wasn't about that," Fitz said.

"Anything else is really going to have to wait, Fitz," she said with a tired sigh.

"You're really worried," he said. He knew he was right. Those lines on her face that were usually all but invisible were deeply etched at the moment.

"I am," she said. "This couldn't be happening at a worse time."

"Maybe that's precisely why it's happening," Fitz said. Then added, "I assume we're talking about the murder?"

"Of course that's what we're talking about," she said, but distractedly.

"I wouldn't think the death of a diplomat would matter so much as all that," Fitz said. "Aside from the bare fact of it, which is terrible enough. But you sound like it somehow means so much more than that."

"It does," she said. "There is going to be a fallout from this. I don't know what, I just know it's going to be overwhelming."

"Really? Heidi Lavatar was so new in her position," Fitz said.

"It reflects badly on your father. The fact that it happened here is bad enough. But she's the second..." she broke off, giving him a pleading look.

"Diplomat Ritchie didn't die," Fitz said.

"We don't know that he didn't," she said.

"We don't know that he did. Legally, he's still considered missing," Fitz said.

"That's not going to matter," she said. Fitz started to object again, but she cut him off. "This isn't about what's true legally. It's about what's true politically."

"I hate politics," Fitz grumbled. Then he gave her a pointed look. "*You* hate politics."

"I do," she agreed with a soft laugh. But then her face was grave again. "But your father was born to it. And I'm afraid one day it's going to be your turn too."

"I try not to think about that," Fitz said drily.

"Hopefully it's decades in your future," she said, then looked around the kitchens with a sigh. "I'm very busy here getting lunch ready for our guests. If you don't need anything from me, I'll get back to it."

"No, but you're right. I should get dressed before I go looking for father," he said. It was getting close enough to lunchtime for his state of undress to be something even Fitz couldn't tolerate.

His mother smiled at him, then started to turn to go. But then she turned back around to say, "but tell me, how is Ritchie doing?"

"As well as can be expected under the circumstances," Fitz said. But he couldn't leave it at that. "I told her everything. About what happened with her father. At least, all I know about it."

"That's why you're looking for your father?" she guessed, her face unreadable.

"I wanted to make a full confession," he said.

Then her hands were on the sides of his face, pulling his head down low enough for her to plant a kiss on his forehead. "I know your father will be angry with you, and you'll have to face up to that. But for my part, I'm pleased you chose the path of honesty."

"Seriously?" Fitz said. This certainly threw a wrench into his assumptions about how his parents were two parts of one thinking whole. "You're not angry?"

"Only a little, that it took you so long," she said.

"But telling her meant going against father," he said. "Something you've always told me to never, ever do."

"Well, sometimes that's the best way," she said with a wry grin. "Not always, not even often, but sometimes."

"Sure. On rare occasions," Fitz agreed with a grin of his own.

She gave his cheek one last affectionate pinch, then got back to work directing her staff. He could already smell white fish grilling up to golden perfection, and the riot of greens, reds, oranges, and purples of the vegetables being chopped up for the salads looked crisply refreshing.

Fitz ran back up to his rooms, taking the back way to his bedroom so he could shower and get dressed before joining the others in the sitting room.

But when he finally emerged from his bedroom, he found only Wyss still there.

"Where are the others?" he asked.

"Ritchie and Moreau are searching their room for clues," Wyss said. "Sokolov is helping. Not that I think they'll find anything. The investigators were all over it before they even came in to talk to Ritchie."

"Of course they were," Fitz said under his breath.

Wyss didn't set his tablet aside, but he did lower it long enough to fix his pale blue eyes on Fitz. "You told her everything?"

"Everything I knew to tell," he said.

"And how's that sitting with you?"

Fitz took a breath, but after holding it for a moment, he just had to let it all rush out of him again, shaking his head. "I really don't know."

"I see," Wyss said. He was still looking at Fitz and not his tablet.

"Why? Did Ritchie say something after I left?"

"Not really," Wyss said, and resumed scrolling through his tablet. "If anything, I would say the two of you didn't finish your conversation. You left things unsaid that should've been said."

"Well, when isn't that true?" Fitz grumbled, but Wyss didn't answer.

There was a flurry of noise as Ritchie, Moreau and Sokolov came back into the sitting room, chatting with each other but falling silent when they saw Fitz there.

"Well?" Fitz said.

"Nothing," Moreau said, but only after several seconds ticked by with Ritchie saying nothing at all.

"It was always a long shot, right?" Fitz said. Then slapped his hands together so loudly they all jumped. "Right! There's only one thing left to do."

"What's that?" Ritchie asked. Her tone was trapped between curiosity and skepticism, and her carefully blank expression wasn't cluing him in at all.

"We need to go to the scene of the crime," he said.

"Wait, the diplomat house?" Sokolov asked.

"Ritchie's childhood home? That diplomat house?" Moreau asked.

They were both glaring at him darkly, like he was being supremely insensitive. But he didn't think he was. Ritchie knew how to conduct an investigation. It was only remarkable they had waited so long to do this.

But maybe this was a crime she didn't really want to solve herself. Maybe for once she wanted it over and done with, without any personal involvement from her.

"That is, if Ritchie agrees?" Fitz said.

Ritchie looked up at him as if he had caught her dozing off. Then she looked around at the others, all watching her closely.

"Well, of course," she said.

"Unless you wanted to wait until after lunch?" Fitz asked. "Fish fresh from the river, vegetables from the gardens. I have no idea what the dessert is."

"As lovely as that all sounds, another formal meal is the very last thing I want," Ritchie said, finally letting genuine emotion show.

"We can grab something when we get back," Fitz said. "It's been years since I've raided *these* kitchens."

She didn't smile at his little joke, but that was all right. She was surely worried about facing her childhood home and a murder scene both at once.

But they'd all be there with her. She wasn't going through it alone. Not if Fitz had anything to say about it.

9

IT WAS a short walk from the administrative building that was Fitz's home to the little cottage that had once been Ritchie's. There were several rolling hills between, enough to tuck the cottage out of sight from even the vantage point of the balconies on the top floor, but it was still so short a walk that Ritchie could well remember the many times she had traversed it at a dead run.

Not that they took it at any kind of a hurry. None of them seemed that eager to get to a crime scene. Instead, they strolled along the gravel path through the grasslands, soaking up the warmth of the midday sun and listening to the many birds that called to each other, most unseen but a few perched precariously atop blades of grass that didn't look strong enough to support even their tiny weight.

The scent of the Immerweis was stronger, closer to the diplomat's cottage. Their blooms dotted the grassland all around the eastern sides of the hills, in some places so thick they looked like clumpy snow. The perfume of it was almost too intense when the air was still. But the day was fortunately a breezy one.

"This is it?" Moreau asked as the path emerged from between two more hills and the cottage at last came into view. "It's so small."

"It's big enough," Ritchie said.

"We spent most of our time outdoors," Fitz said. "But look, Ritchie. Your mother's kitchen garden is still there."

She saw what he was pointing to, the rows of plants that flanked the cottage's back door. Beans were growing up poles, shading the baby gourds that would be massive come harvest time. A variety of herbs were arranged in raised beds, and beyond those were the tomato and pepper plants.

She would have to tell her mother about it the next time she messaged her. Since the day they had left so suddenly, never to return, her mother generally didn't mention Buennagel or their time there. But the closest she had ever come was lamenting not being able to have a garden of her own on the space station. The greenhouse space was all used by the station administration for the good of all. No one could claim even the tiniest of private plots.

Of course, that would mean explaining to her mother that she was on Buennagel. Leaving Oymyakon had happened so suddenly, she hadn't had a chance to bring her mother up to date.

But that wasn't entirely true, was it? Because she had sent Guy Travert several messages updating *him* on what she was about to do. All of which went unanswered. At least she had broken that habit since arriving. He had made it very clear their relationship was over. It was time for her to put it in her past, too.

"You all right?" Moreau asked.

"Yeah, just thinking about my mom," Ritchie said. Moreau gave her a skeptical look, but said nothing.

Sokolov and Wyss had run ahead of the others, but now they were coming back around the corner of the cottage. "There's a barrier across the front door," Sokolov said.

"What kind of barrier?" Fitz asked.

"Physically? Just a strip of tape," Wyss said. "Electronically, there's an alarm system. Any unauthorized person entering the premise will trigger a notification to the security teams."

"How hard is it to make us authorized?" Fitz asked.

"Didn't we agree to stop asking Wyss to do illegal things?" Ritchie reminded him.

He blinked at her, and she really couldn't say if he was confused or only pretending to be confused. "Did we?" he asked.

"You can ask me anything you like," Wyss said. "I choose what I agree to."

"So, do you agree to this?" Fitz asked sheepishly.

"I've already given us the low level clearance that will let us inside the house," Wyss said. "We'll have to go in through the kitchen door, though. The bedroom, which is the actual crime scene upstairs, requires a higher security clearance to access. If we really need it, I can give us that too, but it's going to draw attention."

"Let's just see what the rest of the house shows us first," Ritchie said.

She led the way to the kitchen door, brushing past the out-stretched branches of the tomato plants as she did so. She was just lamenting how that sharp scent was going to cling to her all day now when she opened the door and was struck by a wall of dark, coppery smell.

"Blood," she said, stepping back from the doorway with a hand to her nose. "There must've been a lot of blood."

"That, plus the house is all closed up," Wyss noted.

"Do you want to back off?" Fitz asked Ritchie.

Ritchie shook her head. "I just wasn't ready for it. I'll be fine." She took one last deep breath of garden air, then plunged into the darkness of her childhood home.

Wyss was right; the entire place was sealed up tight. Not only were all the windows closed against the warmth of the breeze, the shutters had been fastened too. When she was a girl, they had only done that when a particularly violent storm was on its way. With them closed, the interior of the cottage was a dark collage of gray patches against more numerous spots of inky blackness.

The air was still and cold, and the smell was so overwhelming she expected to see blood everywhere. But there wasn't a hint of it anywhere in the kitchen or in the great room beyond. The entire bottom floor was one open space, and not a very large space at that. Even in the darkness, she knew she wasn't missing seeing anything.

But she could still hear the birds outside, chittering and singing in the grass. It sounded so far away.

"All right?" Moreau asked her again.

"Yeah, there's nothing down here really," she said, turning to see they were all in the kitchen with her now, although Sokolov had left the door open behind her. Probably not by accident, Ritchie guessed. The sight of that garden bathed in sunlight was a balm as she moved deeper into the shadows of the cottage.

The furnishings were almost entirely unchanged since her time there. The same heavy dining table sat just off the end of the slate tiles of the kitchen floor, resting on the scuffed and faded bamboo flooring that dominated the rest of the house. The stuffed chairs and sofa in the living room area were the same pieces as she had sprawled out on as a kid, but they were arranged differently. Her parents had always kept them circled around a low central table, but that table was gone and two of the chairs were tucked under a west-facing window while the other chair and sofa faced the east-facing window.

"I'm guessing neither of the diplomats since my father had families that lived with them," Ritchie said.

"No, that's right," Fitz said. "The fellow who took the position after your father was abducted was a widower who came out of retirement at my father's strong persuasion. And Heidi Lavatar had not yet been married."

"I want to go upstairs," Ritchie said.

"I don't know," Fitz said warningly. "Didn't Wyss say that was the higher clearance area?"

"Just the larger of the two bedrooms," Wyss told him. "The smaller bedroom and the bathroom are open to us."

"They're probably open because there are no clues there to what happened here," Sokolov said.

"I know. You're right. I just want to take a quick look at my old bedroom," Ritchie said.

Fitz moved closer to her in the artificial twilight and asked, "did you want me to go up with you?"

Ritchie bit her lip. Could he honestly not tell how hard she was working to not scream at him nonstop? Didn't he see how upset she still was from the night before? But she had to shelve all those feelings for the sake of this investigation.

Only going up to her room wasn't about that. She doubted there were any clues in there. She just wanted to see it. But whatever feelings it unleashed in her, Fitz was the very last person she wanted to share those with. Not now. Not yet.

"I'll go up with you," Moreau said, brushing Fitz aside to catch hold of Ritchie's hand.

"Fine," Fitz said, far too brightly. "The rest of us will have a more thorough look down here while you're up there. All right?"

"Whatever," Ritchie said, and she and Moreau climbed the steep stairs to the smaller second floor. There was a small landing halfway up, then the stairs turned back to continue on to a short hallway with just three doors. The door on the left was closed, but the other two stood open.

"This is so weird," Moreau said.

"What do you mean?" Ritchie asked. "The murder is bothering you? We've seen worse than a closed door, you know."

"I know. I meant just how small this place is," Moreau said. "All of it together isn't the size of Fitz's sitting room. His personal sitting room, from when he was a kid."

"I suppose most of your friends have homes more like Fitz's?" Ritchie guessed.

"Most have far larger homes," Moreau said.

"Wait, how big is your room?" Ritchie asked. "Bigger? How can it be bigger?"

"How can it be bigger? You just build it that way," Moreau said with a shrug. "I never gave it a second thought."

"Yeah, but you knew I didn't come from a family like that," Ritchie said.

"Well, there's knowing and then there's knowing," Moreau said. "For what it's worth, there's a reason when I dragged you away for that semester break, I didn't bring you to my house."

"Afraid I'd get lost forever inside of it?" Ritchie asked. They had reached the open door to her childhood room and before she'd even taken in any of the contents, Ritchie swept an arm over the expanse of it. "This space? Bigger than where my mother, grandmother and I all live back on the space station."

"Yeah, I really can't imagine that," Moreau said. "Our room at the barracks is more than twice as big, and we only sleep there."

"I know. Secretly, I think my mother and grandmother enjoy having me gone. Not that they don't miss me, but without me there, they each get half the room to themselves."

Then she stepped inside the room. Not only was all the furniture still the same and arranged in the same way, with the desk under the window and the bed in the corner, even the bedding was the same.

She opened the drawer of the night table and saw her old tablet still waiting for her. The battery must long since be drained now, but she slipped it into the cargo pocket of her pants all the same. She had mourned its loss when she had finally realized she had left it behind in all the commotion. Now she couldn't even remember what could possibly be on it that had been worth all those tears.

Well, to be fair, those tears struck her constantly for most of that first year. She remembered crying when the pudding she took from the school cafeteria that she thought was chocolate had turned out to be lemon. More than cry, she had sobbed at the bottom of the stairwell for the better part of an hour. And she didn't even like pudding.

"I hate to ask again," Moreau said as she sat down on the foot of the bed, "but are you doing all right?"

"This isn't particularly traumatic, finding nothing has changed," Ritchie said as she slid open the door to the closet. She pointed to a smaller door built high into the back wall of that closet. "See that? It opens onto the roof over the kitchen. I used to go out there to look at the stars. I always thought it was my secret thing, although in retrospect I doubt my parents didn't know."

"I wasn't worried about how the nostalgia was treating you," Moreau said. "Or being accused of murder, either. I'd say by this point you'd be pretty used to that."

"Sadly," Ritchie said, sliding the hidden door open and letting in a blast of sunlight and birdsong. Then she slid it shut again with a sigh. "I know what you're asking me, Moreau."

"I figured you might," Moreau said. "You're clever like that."

"Am I?" Ritchie said with a little laugh. "All I feel at the moment is tired. So very tired."

"You certainly *look* tired," Moreau said.

"Thanks."

"So Fitz told you everything," Moreau said, choosing her words slowly and carefully. "But you and I both know he can be a little oblivious to some things. Did he just blunder in and dump it all out and then walk away?"

"I was the one who walked away," Ritchie said.

"But I got the first part right?"

"Look, I'm trying really hard not to let the anger take over. Because I *am* angry, but now isn't the time to unleash it," Ritchie said.

"Because of the murder case?" Moreau asked.

"No, although that's certainly part of it," Ritchie said. "Mostly I have to back burner the anger for now because I still haven't sorted everything through in my mind. What he told me last night, it was *a lot*. I don't know what it all means or how I even feel about any of it. So I was up all night trying to figure it out, but there just weren't enough hours in the night. And now there's this. Murder."

"If you need space from Fitz and he's not getting your signals on that, I can help out," Moreau said.

"Thanks, but I think he gets it," Ritchie said. "I mean, he's not here now."

"I'm not sure he took your hint so much as mine," Moreau pointed out.

"Fair enough. By all means, keep running interference."

"Oh, I will," Moreau said archly. But then she sobered again. "Seriously, doesn't knowing make you feel even the tiniest bit better? Not about your father, I'm sure. That's a lot. But about Fitz."

"What do you mean?" Ritchie asked.

"Well, now you know why he's been so weird. Not that it excuses some of the things he's done. But now you know he was always doing everything because he thought it was the best thing for you. I'm not saying he succeeded, but that was the underpinning of everything. Right?"

"But don't you see? That just makes it all worse," Ritchie said glumly. "That just means I can't even be angry at him for anything he's done before, because his intentions were good or whatever. None of my feelings were ever valid?"

"I'm not saying that," Moreau hastened to say.

"I know you're not," Ritchie sighed. Then she tapped her own temple. "I'm thinking it. Over and over again. Which only makes me angrier, which is even less valid than my first anger. It's a vicious cycle."

"Trust you to make everything super complicated," Moreau said, getting up from the bed to grasp both of Ritchie's shoulders and stare straight into her eyes. "Feel what you're feeling. And then stop. No more analyzing your own feelings. Just let yourself feel them."

"That's easy to say," Ritchie said.

"Are you kidding me?" Moreau asked. "I said feel your feelings, I didn't say a word about acting on them with impunity. I know that's not going to be easy. But I think it's your first step. Given that sitting in a quiet place alone with your thoughts is just not on the schedule for this trip."

"As much as I need it," Ritchie said. She took one last look around her old bedroom. But there was nothing there for her anymore. She turned towards the door but then stopped there. She didn't dare turn back to face Moreau, but she didn't hold back her words either. "You know what the worst of it is?"

"What's the worst of it?" Moreau asked gently.

"That Fitz really has always valued our friendship more than I have," Ritchie said.

"I don't think I'd agree to that assessment," Moreau said.

But Ritchie carried on with her original thought. "What ever happens next, it has to start from that place. Knowing that fact. And what is that going to mean in the future? When we're at guardian school together, or beyond that?"

Moreau was quiet for a moment. Then she said, "you know, if I didn't know you better, I'd swear you were talking about something besides a friendship."

"But you do know me," Ritchie said.

"Do I?"

"You do," Ritchie said. "I'm just saying… it's complicated."

She was still standing with her back to Moreau, but somehow she could sense the smirk on her buddy's face.

"Come on," Ritchie said. "Let's get back to the others. We've wasted enough time here."

It was time to shift her attention to this murder for real. Because that was something she could sort out and solve. And it would all arrange itself tidily in her mind by the time she was done.

She really needed that feeling right now.

10

FITZ LEANED on the bar that divided the kitchen from the dining area inside the darkened cottage, watching the screen on Wyss' tablet. It was a drone's-eye-view of the exterior of the cottage, more specifically the exterior of the cottage outside the window of the bedroom that was off limits.

"You're sure that's not going to set off the security notifications?" Sokolov asked from behind them. She was searching the kitchen cabinets, as if the murderer had left a clue there. And that the guardian investigators had missed it.

"I promise you it's fine," Wyss said, then he and Fitz sucked in a breath at once.

"Is that blood?" Fitz asked.

"Yeah. It looks like they didn't clean up that room at all," Wyss said.

Somehow, seeing those spatters of scarlet darkening to brown made the coppery smell that permeated the cottage all the stronger again. Fitz looked down at the butcher block surface of the kitchen bar. How many times had he sat here as a kid, eating eggs with Ritchie that her mother scrambled up for them on a cast-iron skillet? Now the thought made his gorge rise.

Well, that was probably because of the smell.

"Can you get in through the window?" Fitz asked, dragging his eyes back to the screen.

"I can open it with a waldo, but I'll have to keep the drone outside," Wyss said, leaning over his controller to finesse those movements. The window opened easily under the drone's touch. They could see further into the bedroom now, the bedroom where Ritchie's parents used to sleep.

But all there was to see was more blood. It had even sprayed up onto the ceiling.

"How can anyone think Ritchie would do a thing like that?" Sokolov asked. "Never in her life could she be that angry."

"I don't know. I've seen her pretty angry," Fitz said. But that attempt at a joke fell flat, and he regretted his words at once.

To his relief, the other two just pretended he hadn't said anything at all.

"I don't think this was done in a hot rage," Wyss said as the drone slowly panned its eye camera from one end of the room to the other. "This looks more like a cold sort of passion. Very precise."

"That looks precise to you?" Sokolov asked, horrified.

"No, I get it," Fitz said, as much as he wished he didn't. "It's a lot of blood. Whoever did this was very careful to cut her deep enough to make her bleed, but he prolonged her death for as long as he could."

"Wyss?" Sokolov asked desperately.

"I agree," Wyss said. "This wasn't a quick death. And whoever did it was very methodical. The security systems were disabled one by one, very subtle work. Nothing that should have alerted either her or the security team up at the administrative building was triggered at all. And they should've been. It shouldn't be possible to do this and not be noticed. But they did it."

"At the very least, that narrows our list of suspects," Fitz said to Sokolov. She nodded, but refused to be cheered.

Footsteps came down the staircase, and they all looked up to see Ritchie and the Moreau rejoining them. Whatever had kept them upstairs for so long, it didn't show on either of their faces. Ritchie looked just as red-eyed and tired as before, no more and no less. And Moreau? Frankly, he could never read her, anyway.

"Anything?" Fitz asked. Ritchie just shook her head.

"Nothing," Wyss said. His eyes were on the tablet as the drone backed away from the window, then lowered down closer to the ground before zipping in the kitchen door. Sokolov caught it midair, then handed it to Wyss, who slipped it into his cargo pocket.

"Well, anyone else hungry?" Fitz asked. "The formal lunch is over by now, which means we can raid the kitchen for leftovers without enraging my mother or having to mingle with the other guests."

"But don't we want to mingle with the other guests?" Sokolov asked. "We still haven't found our contact."

"Dinner is soon enough for that," Ritchie said, sounding as tired as she looked.

They all headed out into the garden and Ritchie pulled the door shut behind them, making sure it was securely latched before they left. Fitz decided not to point out the open bedroom windows above them. He wasn't sure the drone could close them again; it was probably better if she didn't know.

Moreau, Ritchie and Sokolov took the lead, walking briskly back up the path. Wyss was attempting to walk and use his tablet at once. Fitz had seen him do this enough to know he was unlikely to trip, but he slowed his steps to match his buddy's pace all the same.

He didn't mind. Whether it was deliberate or just subconscious, he was sure Ritchie was setting such an aggressive speed because she wanted some space between the two of them. The least he could do was to let her have it.

Plus, it was just a lovely day for a walk. Something they never had on Oymyakon: lovely days. The scent of the Immerweis was overwhelming, but a welcome change from the coppery smell of death inside the cottage. Then a flash of motion in the sky caught his attention, and Fitz looked up to see a trio of people far overhead, riding the thermals in colorful gliders.

He longed to be up there with them, riding the currents of air. He had done enough flying on Oymyakon that he knew he hadn't gotten rusty. He bet he could stay up there until past sundown, riding the cool night sky, watching the light from the twin moons flash across the glider frame.

But he doubted there'd be time for such things. Even if a murder hadn't interrupted their time on his home world, there was just too much to be done.

Like talking to his father. Which was proving more difficult than he ever imagined. Had he always been kidding himself that *he* was the one avoiding *his father* and not the other way around?

One thing he hadn't kidded himself about: he had always known when Ritchie knew the truth, she would be angry. But *was* this anger? She was so cold, so remote. It didn't feel like anger. But he didn't know what it was. All he knew was that they still weren't friends again. Was the anger yet to come?

When he and Wyss finally walked in through the tall double-doors into the front hall, they found Ritchie, Moreau and Sokolov in a cluster at the bottom of the stairs, waiting for them.

"Lunch, right?" Fitz said, pointing up the shorter of the staircases, the one that only led up to the second floor.

"Just a moment, cadets," someone said from behind them. Fitz turned to see four guardians emerging from their command center under the grand staircase. Two of them were the two who had come up to the sitting room that morning, Wahli and Rodin. The other two were strangers to him, and they lacked investigator insignias on their uniforms. Basically, just security guards then. Still, was no one left on staff from his childhood days?

"Can we help you?" Fitz asked. Without even thinking about it, he moved to stand between the four of them and Ritchie, who had stopped midway up the stairs.

"You're free to go, Cadet Fitz. It's Cadet Ritchie we need a moment with," Rodin said. She gestured for him to step aside.

"What's this regarding?" Fitz asked, ignoring her hands even as she repeated her gesture for him to move.

"We got the DNA tests back on that knife," Wahli said.

"And so? She already told you she touched it," Fitz said. "If you don't have more evidence than something that already matches her story, you clearly don't have enough to detain her. If you have questions, they can wait until after lunch."

"Nothing is waiting until after lunch," Rodin said.

"Her DNA was all over the handle," Wahli said. "That doesn't match her story."

As subtly sneering as Rodin was, Wahli at least had a "just doing my job" vibe. Like he didn't believe Ritchie had done it either, but he had to work the case before he could clear her.

If he was the only one there, the hairs on the back of Fitz's neck probably wouldn't be standing on end just now. The other two guardians who only waited patiently outside the command center door didn't seem to have any feelings about the matter one way or the other.

But Rodin was another matter. Fitz wasn't willing to give Ritchie up. Not to her.

"That's not enough evidence to detain her, and you know it," Fitz said. He was just warming up. All of his supporting arguments were already coalescing in his mind, ready to be deployed.

But before he could say another word, his father and Klemm strode into the hall.

"Oh, good," his father said to the guards at the bottom of the stairs. "You've found her."

"Yes, sir," Wahli said.

"We just need her to come along with us quietly, but that doesn't seem to be happening," Rodin said.

The general scowled, then turned his attention to the cadets. He took in the arrangement of their bodies and his scowl deepened as he turned it on Fitz.

"Step aside, son," he said darkly.

"No," Fitz said. "This isn't right."

"Her DNA was found on the weapon," Guardian Wahli told the general. "Her DNA and the victim's. No one else's. That is enough probable cause for us to detain her. By protocol, we have to."

"She didn't do this," Fitz pleaded. But why wasn't Ritchie saying anything? It wasn't like her to take something like this quietly.

"She is only being detained as a person of interest. No one has yet accused her of anything," his father said. Then he belatedly threw a questioning look Wahli's way.

"Yes, sir. That is correct," Wahli said, then gestured for Ritchie to come down the stairs. But the look on Rodin's face was just a little too predatory for Fitz's liking.

"Oh, really?" Fitz barked out a dry laugh. "You know, I heard something similar just a few days ago. When I was detained for days despite never being guilty of anything."

"And was that a hardship for you, son?" his father asked archly.

"It was an injustice I won't stand by and see done to anyone else," Fitz said. "Especially not Ritchie."

"The security systems were hacked," Lieutenant Klemm said, startling everyone in the hall. He seldom spoke above a whisper, but now his voice carried throughout the cavernous space.

"That's true," the general agreed. "It was delicately done. Clearly the work of a professional."

"Come on!" Fitz cried out, throwing up his hands.

"We have proof she's accomplished similar tasks in the past," Klemm said. "We can establish enough similarities between the various breaches to prove to even the least cooperative of judges that she is at least a suspect in this."

Fitz fumed, his hands balling into fists. There was just something about Klemm that rubbed him the wrong way. He wanted to see Ritchie taken away by him even less than he did by Guardian Rodin.

His father was gazing at him steadily, his eyes twitching ever so slightly. Like there was something he was trying to say to Fitz without saying it out loud. Sometimes he and Ritchie could communicate that way, but with his father? Never. He had no idea what his father was trying to convey to him.

Probably to go along quietly and not make a fuss. Not embarrass him. Not disgrace his family. That sort of thing.

But it was all too maddening. At the very least, his father had to know for a fact that those things Klemm was putting at Ritchie's feet had actually been Wyss's doing. Wasn't that why he was Wyss's number one fan?

"Come on," Fitz pleaded. "I know you know—"

But a hand squeezing his shoulder gently asked for his silence. He turned to see Ritchie behind him, shaking her head.

Of course, she wouldn't want to get Wyss in trouble. But didn't she get it? His father would protect Wyss in a way he wouldn't protect her.

"It's all right, Fitz," she said. "This is probably safer for me, anyway."

He didn't believe that for a minute. But the look in her eyes told him how futile it would be to argue with her. He had better chances with his father. And those chances were dismal.

"I'll make this right," he promised her.

Then he stepped aside and watched as she walked down to the guardians, her wrists already out to accept whatever restraints they wanted to put on her.

Somehow, he was going to make this right.

11

RITCHIE LOOKED DOWN at her wrists encased in the security cuffs. They felt strange. When she kept her wrists still, it was like they weren't even there. Or more like they created a negative impression, thin rings around her wrists where the cool air of the entrance hall wasn't touching her skin.

Then she tried moving her hands away from each other, and they tightened viciously, cutting off the circulation to her fingers. She could even smell the acrid scent of the little hairs on her arms burning.

No one around her said a word. The four guardians seemed to be waiting for some signal from the general, but he had lapsed into silence. In fact, he was looking down studiously at the floor between his feet, his hands deep in his pockets.

She knew that posture well. Fitz did it all the time when he was brooding over something.

But "brooding" was never a word she associated with his father. It was disturbing to see, like something in the universe had just gone wrong somehow.

And Fitz, at the bottom of the stairs, was standing in the exact same position. At least with him, it made sense. She knew he didn't like that she had just turned herself in, but she didn't want to make anything more difficult. Not the murder investigation, and definitely not his relationship with his father. Cooperation just seemed like the only way to her.

But he was sulking. Or was he? There was an air about him, like he was as confused as she was by his father's brooding.

"Sir," Wyss said, suddenly breaking the silence and snapping the general back into his more customary commanding posture. "Ritchie can't hack into security systems. Whatever events in the past you're referring to, they would've been my doing."

"I'm aware of your skill level as well as Cadet Ritchie's," the general said gruffly. But he mellowed a bit. "Cadet Ritchie is just being placed under house arrest. She won't be taken into custody. This is safer for everyone."

"Politically?" Fitz asked, not looking at his father.

"Fitz, enough," Ritchie said. Then she held her wrists out towards his father, carefully keeping them close together. She didn't want to repeat that strangling sensation. "Will I have to wear these from now on?"

"No," he said, a thoughtful drawl. Then he looked up at the guardians on either side of her. "Parole her implant, explain what that means to her in detail, then let her go."

"Sir," the guardian named Rodin started to object, but the general glared at her so fiercely she shrank down without a further word.

"Yes, sir," Wahli said, and led Ritchie to where the other two were still waiting at the door to the room under the stairs.

She looked back over her shoulder at the others. The general and Klemm were already leaving the room, heading towards the sound of people gathering in one of the reception rooms deeper in the house. Sokolov was standing on the stairs behind Fitz, her hand on his shoulder as she tried to draw him out of his funk. Wyss and Moreau had come halfway across the hall before being stopped by the guardians. They both gave her the same upthrust of their chins, wishing her strength.

She was going to need it.

"You guys go ahead without me. I'll find you when I'm done here," she said as casually as she could. But Guardian Rodin's grip on her elbow was almost painful as she steered her away from the others before any of them could reply.

Ritchie stepped through the door under the stairs to see a room the size of a closet, dominated by a single workstation flanked with monitors. But the guardian who had preceded her was already opening a door on the far side, and the two herded her down a steep, narrow staircase to the basement level.

She hadn't even known there was a basement level. Even as a kid, when she and Fitz had explored what she thought had been everything, she had never known this was there.

At the bottom of the stairs was a security station the size of a guardian police station for a small city. There were uniformed guardians everywhere, working singly in cubicles or together in glass-walled meeting rooms.

"Friedrich, Ustari, take her to medical and find a tech who can run a parole protocol," Wahli said.

"But we—" Rodin started to object.

"—have work to do," Wahli said firmly. Rodin scowled, and Ritchie could feel how badly she wanted to argue, but Wahli outranked her.

"We've got her from here," either Friedrich or Ustari said. They were both standing behind Ritchie and she couldn't see their name tags.

Wahli's face didn't soften a bit, but there was something in his eyes as he looked at Ritchie one last time that made her feel a little less at sea. Rodin might have already decided that Ritchie was guilty, but Wahli knew the job of a guardian was to gather the evidence. Judges and courts determined guilt and innocence.

Not that he thought she was innocent, necessarily. Only that he was there to make sure her rights were respected. It was something.

Rodin and Wahli disappeared among the maze of cubicle walls, and either Friedrich or Ustari took her arm gently to guide her deeper into the basement, away from the open office space to where there were walls and doors.

Their corridor crossed another lined with security cells arranged around a central watch station, but the two guardians didn't take her down that way. Instead, she was led into what looked like a medical room. There was an examining table in the center of the space, but the guardian guided her to the chair next to the desk that sat under a built-in cabinet.

"The tech will just be a moment," he told her.

Ritchie nodded and tried to smile at his kindness, but inside she was in tumult. Then he stepped out to join his body flanking the door. She would have privacy inside the medical area, but there was no way for her to escape.

They were going to mess with her implant. As much as she had weened herself off of using it for more than the basics for months now, the thought that even those basics would no longer be in her control was nerve-wracking.

At least this time, she was being told ahead of time that they were going to be mucking about in her head. Not that she was consenting to it, really. She had no choice. And they could still do more to it than they told her.

Yes, this whole situation was fuel for more paranoia than she knew what to do with.

A tech came into the room and sat down in the desk chair, but rolled it over to sit knee to knee with Ritchie. She looked young, barely out of guardian school, and she gave Ritchie a reassuring smile.

"You look a little freaked out. Have you heard horror stories?" she asked.

"Not really. Fitz had a parole on his implant when we were on Braga last week, so I know how this works," she said.

"Still nervous, though, right?" the tech asked as she wheeled back to the desk and opened one of the drawers to take out a handheld device.

"Some," Ritchie said, but decided not to explain the rest. Better to just get this over with.

"Fitz… you mean Cadet Fitz? The general's son?" the tech asked conversationally as she tapped at her device.

"Yes. Like me, he was accused of something he didn't do," Ritchie said.

"So you already know that a violation of parole is a black mark on your permanent record even if you are cleared of all charges that necessitated the parole?" she asked, glancing up at Ritchie.

"I'm aware," Ritchie said.

"Per the orders of the general, you are confined to the walls of this structure. You are free to move through the private family spaces as well as the public spaces. He didn't specify any off limits spaces for you. If that changes, you will be informed."

"So I can't go outside?" Ritchie asked.

"Only on the balconies," the tech said.

At least she had already been out to the cottage. For the purposes of revisiting old memories, she had been there, done that. As a crime scene, if there was more to be learned there than they'd gleaned already, she could send one of the others.

But she still felt a pang of loss. And a sudden sense of claustrophobia. Although if one were going to be placed under house arrest, it would be hard to find a larger home to do it in.

"All done," the tech said.

Ritchie blinked. "I didn't feel anything."

"Do you usually?" the tech asked.

"I thought something would feel different," she admitted.

The tech glanced at her handheld. "You have almost every working function of your implant on standby mode. That's probably why you didn't notice the change."

"Right," Ritchie said.

"In addition to being physically confined to this building, your use of your implant's search and communication functions will be monitored. You will be warned if you attempt to do something your monitor deems inadvisable, so don't worry about blundering into a mistake."

"My monitor? Someone is assigned to just watch me?"

"There will be a rotation of guardians assigned to keep a passive eye on your doings, but anything that triggers the parole will draw their immediate attention. Don't test it."

"I don't intend to," Ritchie said.

"Good. Any more questions?"

"No," Ritchie said, looking down at her cuffs.

"They'll remove those when they let you go upstairs," the tech told her. "I hope to see you back soon to have that parole removed."

"Yeah, me too," Ritchie said.

Then the tech left and the guardians at the door came back into the room to help her to her feet. Now that she was face to face with them and paying attention, she saw the taller, dark-haired one was Friedrich, and the shorter blond one was Usteri. Usteri took her elbow to guide her back out of the room, and she recognized his gentle yet firm grip from before.

They brought her back up to the grand entrance hall, and Friedrich took off her restraining cuffs.

"You're free to go from here," he told her. "Anywhere in the building, that is."

"Understood," Ritchie said. She debated thanking them, but that felt weird. Sure, they could've all been as unpleasant as Rodin, but did she really have to thank them for treating her like a human being?

But what would it hurt, to be grateful? Because she was grateful.

Before she had quite made up her mind, the two of them were gone behind the door again, and she was alone.

The massive double doors of the front entrance still stood open, letting in the outside breeze. Although facing north, very little sunlight came in with it. But she could see that sunlight dancing over the waves of grass and flowers.

It looked so very far away.

Ritchie figured the others had gone ahead with the plan to raid the kitchens for a late lunch, but she had no appetite. She decided to head to the back of the house, to the smaller family staircase that would take her up to her room. She almost changed her mind when she saw that she'd have to pass the open doors of the reception room where the other guests were gathered. But they were laughing and chattering so loudly with each other she was sure she could slip past unnoticed.

She opted not to pass the doors on tiptoe, or to run. But she did hug the far wall and quicken her steps at least a little. Even so, she couldn't resist the urge to peek inside.

She caught sight of Klemm first, standing in a tight cluster of older people in guardian uniforms. The ones more or less facing her all had very high ranks marked out on their uniforms. Klemm was speaking with them too earnestly to notice her going by, a fact she was grateful for. She hated how it felt, having him watch her.

Then she felt someone else's eyes on her and looked back over her shoulder to see Fitz's father, the general, gazing at her. He was sitting at a table covered in bright displays while a trio of very eager younger officers attempted to point things out to him, but he wasn't paying them any attention at all at the moment. All of his focus was on Ritchie.

But his eyes were inscrutable. Whatever he was thinking, he was keeping it very firmly to himself. Ritchie's feet stumbled to a halt as she looked right back at him, probing for any sense at all of what he meant, looking at her like that. Was he just the tiniest bit sorry for the injustice of treating her like a suspect?

Or was he, like Fitz, thinking of that other, greater injustice done to her years ago?

She stood there mutely in the corridor for far too long, trying to puzzle out Fitz's father. She only came back to the moment when Klemm appeared suddenly at the general's elbow, redirecting his attention to the table in front of him. The general nodded and asked one of the younger officers a question, but as soon as the officer started to answer, his eyes were back on Ritchie.

And they were as hard and unforgiving as she had ever seen them.

She scuttled on away from the open doorway, running to the private staircase and then up four or five floors before she finally had to slow down to a walk again to take the rest.

What did that mean, that look in Fitz's father's eyes? She wasn't sure. She wanted to think he was sorry, or at least felt a little smidge of regret, but she also knew she always wanted to find the best in people. She had to be careful not to kid herself.

But that second look he had given her, the angry one, that one she knew she wasn't kidding herself about.

He had only looked at her like that when Klemm was there. It was a performance, just for Klemm.

But why? Why put on a show for a junior officer? Was he trying to set some sort of example? Show no mercy to cadets, even the ones who are family or as close as? Or was it something else?

Ritchie really wished she knew.

12

THE RAID of the kitchens had gone well, and they'd brought all their booty up to Fitz's sitting room, but Fitz had no appetite for any of it. The sweet, tart smell of the lemonade should've been particularly tempting, given how thirsty he was from the walk to the cottage and back, but he couldn't be bothered to pour himself a glass. He just stood in the doorway halfway on the balcony, alternating looking in on the others clustered around Wyss and his tablet and looking out over the prairie.

Like he was afraid he'd see Ritchie running away. Or being dragged off. Or, for whatever reason, just ending up far away from him.

The others all perked up at once and he leaned into the room to see Ritchie, red-faced and sweating, bursting into the room. He ran to pour a glass of lemonade for her and thrust it into her hands.

"There's an elevator, you know," he said as she gulped it down.

"I needed the exercise," she said, still breathing hard.

"If you like, I'm sure my father would be happy to order you to run laps," he said.

"I can't leave the building," she said.

"There's a track on the fourth floor," he reminded her, but she was distracted by Wyss looking at her closely.

"They paroled your implant," he said.

"You can tell that just by looking at me?" she asked. She sounded appalled at the thought.

"No, I'm in the loop on the security feed, remember?" he said. "How does it feel?"

"It doesn't feel like anything at all," she said with a shrug. "Aside from not being allowed to leave the building, this really isn't going to affect me much. I already barely ever use it."

Wyss gave her a slow nod, but Fitz knew they were thinking the same thing. Ritchie was putting a positive spin on it, but she was troubled. And who wouldn't be? He had hated it himself.

"You have it set to minimum functions?" Wyss asked her.

"Always," she said.

"Why?" Fitz asked Wyss. Because despite her answer, the younger cadet looked troubled.

"They could be monitoring us through her," Wyss said. "Technically, they aren't supposed to. But it's very easy to declare they had a good reason to."

"Well, we were already being careful about what we say," Fitz said.

"Still, I'm going to..." But Wyss trailed off, shaking his head firmly at Fitz before he could even ask what was going on.

Fitz tried to look back to Ritchie, but she was already gone, sitting on one of the sofas with Moreau and Sokolov. Wyss went back to his original position and started pounding away at the keyboard of the communications tablet. Fitz moved around to the back of the sofa to read over Wyss' shoulder.

Of course. He was messaging Hansen to let him know about the implant. Their conversations with Hansen were definitely something they didn't want the security team to eavesdrop on, whether on purpose or even just accidentally.

A response came back almost at once. IT'S FINE. STANDBY.

"Hansen is calling," Wyss announced to the others. They all looked up just as the colonel's face appeared once more on the screen. Again they saw his lips moving, his face grave, but had to wait several minutes for his voice to reach them.

"Security protocol delta-five-five. Sub-protocol gamma-gamma-seven. Authorization Ieuan Hansen, Colonel and instructor, Oymyakon Foreign Service Academy. In loco parentis for Cadet Murdina Ritchie."

They all looked at each other, not certain what that all meant or if they were supposed to say something back.

But then the colonel spoke again. "There, Wyss. That takes care of your concern. Legally, anyone snooping has to back away at this point. We're as free to speak as we ever are."

There was another pause before he continued on. "I was contacted moments ago in regards to Ritchie's parole. I have the basics of that situation. Her mother and grandmother appointed me her legal guardian in this manner, so I am the one who will be contacted first if there is a violation. Which, I trust, there won't be."

Now the pause was clearly an expectant one, but Moreau had to nudge Ritchie before she sat up straighter on the sofa and said, "yes, sir. I mean no, sir. There won't be any trouble."

They waited for her words to reach Hansen, then watched him listen and then respond in that same visually distorted, completely silent way. Finally, they could hear his voice again.

"Very good, cadet. Now, I understand there was a murder. Do you have any leads?"

Fitz bit back a sudden urge to laugh. But of course he knew already. The charges against Ritchie would've been part of the information he had already received, and the rest he could sense on his own.

"Nothing, really. Sorry, sir," Fitz said. Then he looked down at Ritchie. "Unless you have something I don't know about?"

Ritchie twisted her hands together. "No. I had a theory that didn't pan out. We're back at square one. We know the means but not the motive or even who had the opportunity."

"I might have something that speaks to motive, actually," Fitz said. "When I spoke to my mother this morning, she was very worried about the political fallout of the murder. Which seems odd to me. Granted, special diplomat to Buennagel is a prestigious post, but Heidi Lavatar was very new to it. And very new to diplomacy as a whole. I can't imagine she's even had time yet to acquire any enemies, let alone political ones."

They watched as, in agonizing slowness, their words reached Hansen. He nodded at first, acknowledging Ritchie's words, and seemed about to speak, but stopped again. Now he was listening to Fitz speak, and the grave expression on his face turned darker still.

Then he spoke to them earnestly. His words were brief, but they had to wait twice as long for the audio to reach them.

"That is worrying. I will look into it on my end and get back to you. In the meantime, do try to keep your noses clean and your eyes open."

"Sir, was Diplomat Lavatar our contact?" Moreau asked.

Another agonizing wait for his response, but at least they could see him shaking his head no before they heard him say it.

"No, she was not. Your contact is still there among you, waiting for the moment to connect with you. Be patient and be vigilant. I wished I could tell you more, but you just have to sit tight. Understood, cadets?"

He had asked that question minutes ago, his time, but the Hansen on the screen was still watching them all with patient expectation.

The very last thing Fitz wanted to do was wait. Wait and keep secrets. He had had enough of both. But the others were already nodding, even Ritchie.

"We'll be good, sir," Fitz said. Then he couldn't help himself. He had to inject at least a measure of levity into the proceedings. "Even Ritchie, sir."

But once again Hansen cut off the connection without warning, leaving the five of them on their own.

"Right, dinner is in a couple of hours," Fitz said, finally giving in and pouring himself a glass of lemonade. "We never quite compared notes from the first dinner. We should probably do that now and decide how we're going to approach our next opportunity."

"I'm not going to be much use," Ritchie sighed. "I only spoke with Diplomat Lavatar and General Fitz, and that's two people we can definitely cross off the list of potential contacts."

"I spoke with a group of delegates from the non-human caucus of the Union of Free Worlds parliament," Wyss said.

"That's who they all were?" Fitz asked.

Wyss nodded. "I upgraded their translation devices with a program I picked up when we were on Jorda. It has more pheromone and nonverbal communication capabilities. They were quite pleased. But none of them seemed interested in me beyond that."

"I spoke with the son of the head of the isolationist party," Moreau said.

Fitz almost spit out a mouthful of lemonade. He caught himself just in time, but what he swallowed down was as much bitter bile as tart and sweet lemonade. "Head of the what now?" he asked, wiping at his tearing eyes.

"It's new," Sokolov said with an unhappy sigh.

"And the Berwegers?" Fitz asked.

"Are part of it," Moreau confirmed. "Gwer Meckes—that's the boy's name—was a bit wary of me at first. Apparently, I have the reputation of being a friend of Finn and Feena." She rolled her eyes dramatically.

"And he didn't like that?" Ritchie asked.

"Well, he wasn't going to come out and say it, but he clearly has a strong desire to avoid those two," Moreau said. "I told him how they used me, and he had a similar experience with them when he was about ten. Nothing like having your mind invaded and your emotions controlled for you to really put you off of a certain pair of twins, no matter how empirically gorgeous they might be."

Fitz nodded his hearty agreement, but Ritchie just looked down at her lap, her cheeks that had only just gone back to their normal color after her run up the stairs once more bright scarlet.

Finn Berweger had kissed her. Fitz didn't think he was being conceited when he figured that Finn had done that to stick it to Fitz. Which he didn't imagine Ritchie appreciated one little bit. Even if it hadn't ended with her boyfriend also catching an eyeful and bailing on their whole relationship.

Not that he knew what she was feeling. He hadn't said a word to Ritchie about any of that, and she certainly hadn't been in the mood to share with him.

And not that he was anxious to know. At all. He had spent enough time with Feena to know how personal feelings around the Berwegers had a way of becoming complicated. Like intricate math equations, no one has yet solved after centuries and generations of mathematicians having a go at it.

Fitz shook his head to clear those thoughts then asked, "did you get anything useful out of… Gwer, was it?"

"He might be useful in the future," Moreau said. "His father is nominally the leader of the party that the Admirals Berweger are running behind the scenes. He still lives at home on Jorda. Goes to a day school. He sees a lot."

"You should probably bond with him again tonight, then," Ritchie said, still picking at a loose thread on the seam of her pants.

"Yeah. You want to hang with me?" Moreau offered, finally noticing just how bothered Ritchie was.

But Ritchie shook her head. "No, we should split up and cover more territory. There are a lot of people we haven't talked with yet."

"Yeah, I'll be on new people duty myself," Fitz chimed in. Because, useless as he was, he had talked to no one the night before. "Sokolov, did you speak to anyone of interest?"

"Your mother, quite by accident," she said, her cheeks pinkening.

"Please tell me she didn't share any embarrassing stories about me," Fitz said earnestly.

"No, not at all!" Sokolov said. "But the people she was speaking with were all old friends of hers. Some were husbands or wives of other generals, and some were generals and admirals in their own right. But they weren't talking shop. In fact, they were…" she broke off with a nervous laugh.

"What, gossipping?" Moreau asked.

"No, they were talking recipes," Sokolov said. "I gather they have some sort of competition amongst themselves. Like a cooking scavenger hunt. The latest challenge—set by the husband of an admiral who wasn't there, as I gather they weren't supposed to be discussing it and were being quite hush-hush about it all—was to find the best recipe for preparing something called oulu."

"What's oulu?" Fitz asked.

"A fruit from Garovla. I gather it's very fibrous and more peppery than sweet. It was proving quite a challenge. Your mother thinks she's got a winner in a recipe that uses only a small of zest, but the others were sure she'd be disqualified for using such a minimal amount in what's basically a spice cake."

"Huh," Wyss said. At first, none of them were sure what he was referring to, since he was usually more engrossed in whatever was on his tablet than on any conversation he was technically a participant in. But he was looking right at Sokolov when he said it. Fitz guessed he was just stumped at the whole concept of recipe scavenger hunts.

"Maybe I should find new people tonight too," Sokolov said, flushing an even deeper shade of rose.

"Maybe not," Moreau said brightly. "Those people could be like Gwer Meckes. They could be useful contacts to have in the future."

"Contacts for what?" Sokolov said.

"Information," Fitz said simply. "They are people who know things. They could be good friends to have. In the future, when things get worse, we're going to need all of those we can spare."

"Why would they tell me anything important, though?" Sokolov asked.

But this time, it was Ritchie who answered. "We don't have questions now, but someday we will. We need to establish the friendships now."

"They're all so much older than me," Sokolov said. "What do I bring to such a relationship?"

"Enthusiasm?" Fitz ventured.

"But also, intergalactic experience," Moreau added. "You travelled on the railway for more than a year, right? You must've seen so much more than Lady Fabron's blood-cherry cake."

Sokolov sat pensively for a moment. Then a slow grin spread across her face. "You know, you're right? The passengers in the VIP cars always had special requests. Foods from their home worlds, foods from places they had vacationed years ago, foods that were the current trendy must-trys. But you all really think I should stick with that group?"

"Absolutely," Fitz said. "And Wyss, check in with the alien caucus members again. There might just be cultural differences that are making the connection slower. We don't know that our contact is human, after all. All species attend schools on Braga, or even teach there."

"Right," Wyss said with a nod.

"Ritchie and I will mingle with those we missed last night," Fitz said. Just saying her name out loud was making his throat tighten up a little.

She still wasn't looking at him. She still wasn't ready to really talk with him.

"Separately, of course," he added.

"Of course," she agreed. Too quickly.

But perhaps that was for the best. He still had his father to pin down.

If only there was some way to physically pin Klemm down in another room for just five minutes.

                                  13

RITCHIE NOTICED two things about the pre-dinner reception party
pretty much the moment the five cadets walked in the door together.

The first was that it was the most awkward, uncomfortable gathering of people she could ever recall attending.

And the second was that with the exception of the now-deceased
Diplomat Lavatar, everyone who had been there the night before was
there again. And at the governor's house on Buennagel, that was
extremely unusual. Visitors came, visitors left. Some stayed for more
than a day, sure, but never once was it every single one of them. And
no one new arriving? That wasn't something she had ever seen before,
either.

Basically, everyone who had been at the dinner party the night
before was under house arrest, not just Ritchie. She would bet the only
difference was that she also had had her implant paroled. But from the
grumbling around her, she guessed no one was particularly happy
about being detained.

It might have made her feel better, that she wasn't the only one
considered a potential suspect. But there were nearly fifty people in
that reception room, not including everyone on staff in the building.

That was far too many suspects. It had been nearly an entire day already. Had the inspectors seriously not eliminated anyone yet?

But at least the food was good. Although that probably wasn't an accident either. The few times she had caught the eye of Fitz's mother, she could tell that Luana Fitz was working overtime to make sure everyone's involuntary stay was as nice as she could make it. The bacon-wrapped water chestnuts and shrimp were a deliciously salty start.

Ritchie picked up another skewer of shrimp and looked around the room again. They were all supposed to be hunting for their contact again. And she wouldn't object to getting to the killer faster than the security team was seeming to be doing it. But where to start? The guests were gathered in conversational clusters much like the night before, but the conversations they were having were all low and grumbling, quick to drop away at the approach of a stranger.

The whole evening looked like it was going to be another bust.

"I see you favor the shrimp. Of course, you always did as a child as well, as I recall. You and Fitz hiding under the tablecloths, snatching things off of trays when you thought no one was looking. An entire table setting of shrimp cocktails it was that one time, wasn't it?"

Ritchie dry-swallowed the last bit of shrimp and turned to see Fitz's father looking down at her. Glowering, of course. And there was Lieutenant Klemm, just at his elbow. His face was blank, expressionless, but those eyes just made her feel… oily.

"Yes, sir," Ritchie said. She wasn't even sure she remembered the party he was referring to, but it sounded plausible. And who was she to argue with the general?

But his scowl just deepened. How was that the wrong answer?

Then a gong sounded, summoning them all into the dining room for the main event. And the general took her by the elbow.

She was getting really tired of being steered around by her elbow.

"Sir?" Klemm said, almost reproachfully.

"We agreed with security to recreate last night, correct? That includes place settings, Klemm," he said.

"No, it only matters that everyone is…" Klemm started to say, but broke off with a flush and finished with a barely audible, "yes, sir."

It was a relief when he disappeared, but that only meant Ritchie was once more stuck alone with the general at the head of the table.

"Fitz complained quite a bit about his parole," the general said as they both dipped their spoons into a creamy asparagus soup. "I suppose it's less of a hardship for you."

Ritchie let the spoonful of soup linger on her tongue as her mind turned over how she was going to respond to that. What did it even mean? It was less of a hardship for her… why? She was afraid to ask. She could make a guess at a few of the ways she wasn't like Fitz, especially in the eyes of his father. But there wasn't one of them she wanted to say out loud.

"Yes, sir," she said simply, and put a second, larger spoonful of soup into her mouth.

"I understand you have chosen not to be a diplomat," he said. She glanced up at him for as long as she dared, watching him sipping at his soup. But his face was inscrutable to her.

"I didn't so much choose not to be a diplomat as choose to be a guardian," Ritchie said. Then quickly added, "sir," instantly realized how that belated honorific made her sound just like Fitz, and felt her cheeks flush hotly.

"I suppose that's true," the general said blandly. "But I can't help but wonder what led you to that choice?"

"I visited both schools and chose the one that felt like the best fit, sir," Ritchie said.

He narrowed his eyes at her, as if he wasn't sure if she was being sarcastic or not. Given that she had already once unconsciously sounded like Fitz, she couldn't blame him for thinking it was a pattern for her.

"I chose the military path myself, not the path of foreign service," he said, again quite blandly. "But my understanding is that most foreign service cadets already know what they intend to do before they reach their final year and visit the higher schools. This wasn't true in your case?" He tipped his bowl to spoon up the last bit of his soup, then looked at her expectantly as he sipped it off his spoon.

"No, sir. I had to think about it more than most, sir," she said. The server behind her whisked her half-eaten soup away and replaced it with a bowl of brightly colored salad drizzled with a honey-mustard dressing.

"Any particular reason why?" the general asked as he poked at his salad with his fork.

Ritchie jabbed at a chunk of roasted beet, but it kept slipping out from under the tines of her fork. She really needed a few seconds of chewing to think over her response to that, but her salad was just not cooperating. And it was becoming apparent that she was stalling.

"Cadet Ritchie?" the general prompted.

She looked up at him, and there was that look in his eyes again. The one that was never there when Klemm was at his side. Like he was sorry about something?

Was he trying to ask her without asking her if Fitz had already told her everything? But if he wanted to know that, why didn't he just ask Fitz? Fitz, who was dying to tell him.

It didn't make any sense at all. And it left her with no clue as to what she could safely say.

"I've cultivated a wide range of interests and therefore skills," Ritchie said, hoping *that* didn't sound too braggy. "I could see myself pursuing either path. That made the choice take longer for me, I think, sir."

He looked at her intently, chewing on a mouthful of salad thoughtfully. But in the end he just nodded, then turned to speak to the man sitting at his left hand.

Ritchie let out a breath she hadn't even realized she was holding. She was just about to dig into her salad for real when once again it was whisked away from her, replaced by a mixture of vegetables and pasta formed into the shape of a drum. She broke it apart with her fork and was just about to put a bite of it into her mouth when she noticed Fitz on the opposite side of the table and several places down, desperately trying to catch her eye.

How long had he been pretending to brush back his hair so he could wave his hand around like that? She hoped not long. And he stopped the minute their eyes met. He rolled his eyes, then directed them further down the table. Ritchie nodded. She looked down at her food as if the sight of it mesmerized her, but really, she was listening intently. She had to sort out several quieter conversations before she caught the one Fitz had been trying to draw her attention to.

"All I'm saying is that it's my Henri's turn," a woman was saying. She sounded like she had imbibed too much, which was yet another odd thing about this evening. Normally, the servers at the Buennagel governor's house were careful not to let any guest overdo it. The only way it was even possible was if she had gotten started before coming down to the reception, and even then someone should've escorted her out by now. Perhaps with everyone being forced to extend their stays against their will, some of the normal rules were being softened a bit.

But Ritchie had a feeling that was going to be deemed a mistake, and all too soon. She glanced down the table and saw the woman talking was an older woman with blonde hair that wasn't turning so much gray as a brittle kind of yellow. Her cheeks were flushed, and her eyes were bright. And it was in no way clear who at the table she was addressing. But she was speaking loudly enough for it to be any of them.

The man beside her that Ritchie couldn't quite see tried to shush her, but she brushed him away with a scowl. "I won't be quiet. An injustice was done, and I was quiet then. But now there's a chance to rectify it. I won't remain silent now!"

"An injustice? Really?" Fitz asked. "The selection process for such a position is rigidly defined, the findings all public knowledge. The only way the late Heidi Lavatar could've won that appointment was by being the most qualified, despite her age."

"Oh, you're young, dear," the woman said to him, trying to reach across the table to give his hand an affectionate pat but missing by quite a bit. "You'll see when you're older. There's always a way around such things."

The man beside her was trying to shush her again, but he was only darkening the flush of color that stained her cheeks.

"Henri Schor, isn't it?" the general asked from the head of the table. An immediate hush fell over everyone, including the wife of poor Henri. All eyes turned to him and he pushed away from the table to stand. He was a thin man of average height, his hair gray and balding on top, but neatly groomed. He was wearing a diplomat's formal uniform of white and ivory, and gave the general a bow of acknowledgement.

"Yes, sir. Please excuse my wife. I will take her upstairs so she can rest, sir," he said.

"No, there's no need," Fitz's father said. "I'm not so sensitive that I can't hear a bit of criticism, not even at my own table."

Diplomat Schor flushed, and Ritchie felt a spasm of empathy. She wasn't the only one who had no clue how to respond when the general spoke to her.

"I am familiar with your career, Diplomat Schor," the general went on. "It is impressive, to be sure. And you have put in the time. No one can argue with that."

Schor mumbled a, "yes, sir," but Ritchie was sure he felt the "but" coming just as much as she did.

"Diplomat Lavatar was young for such a position, but she had rare talents. Very rare. All too rare. And they were talents I find myself in desperate need of. Her death was a tragedy, her murder a crime that will be paid for. But the loss of her skills, her particular talents, is a blow that strikes me most profoundly of all. I realize that may sound callous or selfish. All I can tell you is that the need for those talents is not mine alone, but is felt by all the Union of Free Worlds."

"And now we are without her," Luana Fitz said from the other end of the table. She looked grief stricken herself. But had she known Lavatar well? Or was this because she, as opposed to anyone else at the table with the possible of exception of Klemm, knew exactly what General Fitz meant?

What could these special, rare talents be?

"We shall fill the position again," Fitz's father said. "But only by another who can perform the duties. I have no use for someone who is merely due their turn."

Diplomat Schor flushed deeply crimson and mumbled another, "yes, sir." But Ritchie felt her own ears flaming as well. The poor man. His wife had embarrassed him enough. Was it really necessary for the general to humiliate him too?

Then the servers swept into the room with the main entrée, and the conversations slowly resumed. Ritchie watched her uneaten appetizer fly out of her reach, but her thoughts were no longer on food.

She turned to the general, and, with a mixture of anxiety and thrill at her own daring, gave him just a hard a glare as he had ever fixed her with.

"What talents are these, if I may ask, sir?" she demanded.

"You of all people don't need to ask me that, Cadet Ritchie," he said. And then Klemm was suddenly there again, leaning over the arm of the general's chair to whisper close to his ear. But even as he whispered to the general, his dark eyes were fixed on Ritchie.

He had heard her question. And she knew that as little as he had liked her asking it, he had liked her demanding tone even less.

The general sighed and wiped his mouth on his napkin, then set it on the table as he rose from his chair.

"I bid you all excuse me. An important matter," he said.

Klemm smirked at Ritchie, and she would swear he had conjured some minor emergency just to deprive her of the general's company. Was he really so deluded to think that would hurt her feelings?

He flounced off to throw open the nearest door, but Fitz's father bent to retrieve the napkin that had tried to follow him away from the table and had fallen to the floor. He set it more firmly next to his plate, and she realized he was lingering so he could meet her eyes one last time.

Again that look. But this time with a side of frustration. He knew whatever he was trying to communicate with her wasn't getting through.

So why didn't he just tell her?

14

FROM WHERE HE had been sitting in the middle of the table, it wasn't too difficult for Fitz to catch everyone else's eye and subtly signal for them to slip away before dessert. Moreau and Sokolov went out first, together, heading towards the bathrooms off the reception room. But once they were out of sight of most of the party, Fitz saw them duck away towards the back elevator.

Wyss went next. It took him a moment to free himself from the conversation of the aliens seated around him. Fitz had no idea what they were all talking about, as they were all using translator equipment to speak each other's languages and not Union standard, even Wyss. But then he too was gone towards the back of the house.

Fitz's father had yet to return, and likely wouldn't, so there was no one at all to notice when Ritchie gave Fitz a nod, then slipped away.

Being in the middle of the table had made signalling the others easier, but getting away himself was a little more difficult. Diplomat Henri Schor and his wife Abilene might have provided a usable distraction, given their continued low-volume arguing, but Abilene seemed to be under the impression that Fitz was on her side. Every time Fitz was just about to slide out of his chair, Abilene would grow louder again, repeating whatever her husband had just said to her and insisting that Fitz surely saw how unreasonable her husband was being.

It was quite annoying.

Then suddenly one of the servers was standing behind him, leaning down to whisper close to his ear. "Cadet Fitz? Will you come with me, please?" she asked formally, then gave the guests around him a smile asking for indulgence.

"Certainly," Fitz said, tossing his napkin on his plate then following the server out to the reception room. The side tables were laden with various desserts about to be deployed in the dining room.

"Here you are," the server said, putting a large tray holding five bowls of spiced chocolate cake with fresh cream and berries. "Compliments of your mother."

"Right. Thanks," Fitz said, taking the tray.

He had never once seen her looking his way or at his friends as they had slinked away, but of course she had noticed. And bailed him out. He would be sure to thank her the next time he saw her.

In the meantime, he carried the tray to the elevator and took it all the way up to the top floor, where he joined the others already gathered in his sitting room.

They had left the lights set to low, but with the gold and the silver moon both nearly full, there was more than enough light for them to see each other. The sound of the crickets carried up from the grasslands below, a slow drone as the evening was on the cool side.

"Compliments of my mother," Fitz said as he set the tray down on the table in the center of the gathering of sofas. To his surprise, it was Ritchie that dove in to seize one first.

"Sorry," she said, putting her hand over her full mouth as she spoke. "Your father was constantly asking me questions. I didn't get to eat a single thing until he left."

"Anything of importance?" Fitz asked.

She thought it over as she chewed and swallowed. "Not about the murder. Or about our contact."

"So it was about…?" Fitz asked leadingly.

"My future," Ritchie said. "Or my past. Whatever. It can wait. Now's not the time." She put another mouthful of cake and cream in her mouth then asked, "what do we think of Klemm?"

"As our contact?" Sokolov asked, looking horrified. "I know what we said about not judging by appearances given Colonel Hansen and all, but I really hope it isn't Klemm."

"Me too," Moreau said. "He creeps me out. He's always watching. Always. I feel like something on a microscope slide every time he's in the room."

"I don't like Klemm either," Fitz said, settling onto a sofa and reaching for a bowl of cake. "But if he works for my father, he was very thoroughly vetted. And given that he works closely with my father, if he had sneaked something past the vetting, I still think my father would catch it. I don't like the guy, but I'd have to guess that he's clean."

"I agree," Wyss said. His eyes were focused on his own bowl, as he systematically removed all the berries and set them on the lip of the bowl, one by one. "But I'd add that I've dug into his official records and everything I could dig up on him. His career is exemplary. He rose quickly through the ranks, but his competency scores and reviews from his superiors back up every promotion he's received. I can find no clue as to any personal political affiliation he might have. I also find no hint of a connection between him and the Berwegers. Or Hansen. I don't think he's our murder. And I'm positive he's not our contact."

"You did all that research just now?" Fitz asked. Wyss had been upstairs ten minutes longer than he had, but somehow that didn't seem implausible to him. Wyss often worked fast.

But Wyss was blushing. "Sorry, I did it after I met him at your family's townhouse on Jorda. He just gave me the creeps. I'm not sure it feels any better knowing there's no reason to feel that way."

"I wouldn't say no reason," Moreau said, setting her empty bowl back on the tray next to Ritchie's. "He's creepy. Feeling creeped out is the appropriate response to that. There's just no box for it on our official records, is there?"

"Actually, there is," Wyss said. "It's just not in the public-facing part of those records."

"Huh," Moreau said, then sat back with a thoughtful look on her face.

Fitz had a thousand followup questions to that little bit of knowledge, but just then that would be chasing the wrong information. "Aside from Klemm, do we have any other suspicions about anyone else being our murderer or our contact?"

"I'm more sure that no one in the alien caucus is either," Wyss said. "They were all alarmed that a murder had happened in a political environment like this place, but that was more a generalized feeling that such a thing, rare as it is, is always alarming. But they have confidence in your father sorting it out. And none of them were trying to get a word with me like our contact would."

"The mood among the recipe-sharing crowd was much the same," Sokolov said. "I guess we have a skewed perspective, actually. Murder has become so commonplace for us on Oymyakon I pretty much forgot how rare it still is in the Union of Free Worlds."

"Especially in a place like this," Ritchie said. "I think you're right, Sokolov. We haven't been taking it seriously enough."

"Is it good news or bad news that Hansen hasn't gotten back to us about the political implications?" Fitz wondered. But none of them had an answer. So he turned to Moreau. "What about Gwer Meckes?"

"He was quiet," Moreau said. "Like, too quiet. Like he'd been told not to talk to me. Because we were told to take our same seats as last night, he had to sit next to me, but I could tell he was intensely uncomfortable, and his parents were watching him very closely."

"He might have overheard something useful, but is too afraid to tell us, then," Fitz mused.

"Or they figured out who we were and chastised him for befriending me last night," Moreau said with a shrug. "If they're tight with the Berwegers, they aren't going to want their only child associating with any of us, their sworn enemies."

"It might be worth trying to pull him aside and talk to him away from his parents at some point," Ritchie said.

"It might," Fitz agreed. "But in the meantime, the Schors."

"Yes, wasn't that interesting?" Moreau said. "And yet somehow I doubt that's what anyone was worried about politically."

"No, their beef was almost bureaucratic," Ritchie said. "And really not even 'theirs.' It felt like only his wife had a problem with Lavatar's promotion."

"Diplomat Schor is perfectly calibrated for the level of responsibility he currently has and no more," Wyss said. They all gaped at him, and he added, "that's what his superiors say about him. It's on his records."

"The unofficial part, I'm guessing," Fitz said.

"The position is open again, but he's not getting it this time either," Wyss said. "Although frankly, I'm not sure who will. Your father nixed dozens of candidates before he chose Heidi Lavatar. And those candidates were pulled from all over the Union. I don't know where they're going to start looking this time."

"Still, Diplomat Schor's wife didn't strike me as someone who knows what her husband's superiors think about him," Ritchie said. "She seems like she truly believes he should've gotten the position. But is she unhinged or just not handling the stress of being trapped here well?"

"I think we should poke around their room while they're still busy downstairs," Fitz said. "Maybe they left some clues lying around."

"Do we suspect them strongly enough to justify that?" Sokolov asked. "Not to mention it sounds risky."

"They seem suspicious enough to be worth a look to me," Moreau said.

"Not just you," Wyss said as he tapped at his tablet. "Ritchie, do you sense that?"

"Sense what?" Ritchie asked, looking back over her shoulder at the empty balcony behind her.

"They made an adjustment to your parole," Wyss said. "You're no longer allowed to move anywhere within the building."

"What? Where are they confining her to? This floor?" Fitz asked. He realized he had jumped to his feet, but he had no idea why.

But Wyss was grinning at him. "She can go anywhere in this building with one exception."

"The Schors' room," Ritchie guessed.

Wyss nodded.

"They must be searching it themselves, then," Sokolov said. But Wyss was shaking his head.

"Why wouldn't they? They just don't want me poking around, that's it?" Ritchie asked.

"They intend to pull the Schors aside after the post-dinner party is over. They'll be questioned, and their permission will be asked before anyone searches the room," Wyss told them.

"Before anyone *from security* searches their room," Fitz said. "We have to move. We don't have much time."

"I'll wait here," Ritchie said, but her voice had a false brightness to it.

"We need all hands to search the room as quickly as possible," Fitz said, but Ritchie just shook her head no. Then she tapped the back of her skull.

"Parole, remember?"

"I can fix that," Wyss said.

"Can you?" Fitz asked. That would've really come in handy when he was paroled on Braga. But Wyss had been stuck on Oymyakon at the time.

"I don't need you to do that," Ritchie said. "The risks are too high, and in all likelihood there's not going to be anything in the Schors' room to even make it worth it."

"It's super simple," Wyss said.

"It's more than my implant tracking, remember? They can see what I see whenever they want to. And only Hansen can countermand that," Ritchie said.

"I can spoof it. It will look like you're right where you are now, in Fitz's sitting room. Even if they look through your eyes," he said.

"I'm sure you can, Wyss," Ritchie said. "But it's not worth risking getting you or me into trouble. You all can search without me. I'll find something useful to do while I wait, I promise."

"I don't want to do this without you," Fitz said. He didn't add the rest. How it wouldn't be any fun without her, because he knew how much she'd hate that. That he wasn't taking the murder seriously. He *was*. But he also loved solving crimes.

But not without her.

"It's not up to you, Fitz," Ritchie said. She didn't look at him, but her tone was harsh enough. Her words hit him like daggers.

"Fine," Fitz said. "Are the rest of you coming or what?"

But he didn't wait for an answer. He just strode out of his room and into the darkened interior corridor that led to the elevators.

"Tenth floor," Wyss told him as the four of them piled into the elevator. Fitz jabbed at the button, then noticed Moreau giving him a look.

"What?" he all but snapped.

"You know what," she said.

Fitz pointed back towards his sitting room. "She's the one being unreasonable, not me."

"Gee, I wonder why?" Moreau said sarcastically.

"The three of us can do this on our own if you want to go back and talk to Ritchie," Sokolov offered.

"No, let's just get this done. Solve the murder. Get on with our lives," Fitz said. Sokolov looked away as she nodded, and he realized his brusque words had hurt her feelings. But he couldn't bring himself to apologize.

Even if he went back to talk to Ritchie, what could he possibly say to her? Nothing different from what he had said before.

It wouldn't make any difference.

15

RITCHIE STACKED ALL the empty cake bowls together and carried them over to the replicator in the corner of the room to be recycled into raw matter. Then she did the same with the spoons, and lastly, the tray itself.

And then she officially ran out of useful things to do.

She wandered out to the moonlit balcony. She had intended to stand at the railing and look down at the calming waves of grass again, but instead she found herself pacing back and forth, back and forth as she waited.

She told herself for the umpteenth time that searching the room of an only mildly suspicious couple was absolutely not worth putting her future career in jeopardy, let alone Wyss's. She knew it wasn't.

But she really wished she was down there now, helping the others search.

Only it was so hard, being in the same room as Fitz. It was all so confusing.

He had always known the truth about her father. That sentence just kept ringing through her mind, over and over again. He had always known the truth about her father. And he had never said a word to her. Not even a hint.

And no matter what he thought, suddenly telling her the truth wasn't all it took for them to be friends again. That didn't instantly win her trust. Especially as she still didn't know the whole story.

But focusing on Fitz's betrayal was a strangely comforting sort of anger. She was used to being annoyed and even angry with Fitz. She knew how to live with those feelings.

But not knowing what exactly happened that day with her father was the vast, bottomless sea of darkness that lurked under that surface anger with Fitz. Had he been set up? By Fitz's father? Why? And what did it mean now that she knew? Was she a target, too?

What about her mother and her grandmother?

Ritchie hugged her arms tight to her sides, realized she was doing this because she was shaking, and quickly forced her mind back to Fitz. Fitz trying to make everything better with one simple gesture. Like it could ever be that easy.

She really wished she was with him now, searching that room.

"Ritchie?" Fitz called, and she ducked back inside the sitting room just as Fitz turned the lights up to full. She blinked at the sudden brightness, then jumped back as something clattered to the ground at her feet.

"What's all this?" she asked as she danced back from a pile of swords and knives that flashed in the lights as they rocked on the tiles.

"Look familiar?" he asked her, grinning wildly.

"They look like the ones from our room," Moreau said, then added with deep sarcasm, "*kind of.*"

Ritchie dropped to one knee to look at them closer, not letting her fingers get anywhere near any of them. "It's a similar set. Long sword, short sword, curved dagger," she said.

"The markings are similar as well," Sokolov said, but she, like Moreau, was far less excited by this find than Fitz.

"They share a homeworld," Wyss told her, "but the dating is centuries apart. And at any rate, none of it means anything, since they all technically belong to the Buennagel Governor's Residence Collection. Not even to your father. Technically."

"Did you think this was a clue?" Ritchie asked Fitz. She couldn't help herself. She smiled just a little. But it was hard not to be amused, how eager Fitz was to show her something that meant nothing at all.

"It's a pattern," he insisted. "Maybe they killed the diplomat with one of these, then swapped out the dagger to pin it on you. Or something."

"But the sets have widely divergent provenances," Wyss said firmly.

"Yeah, I'm afraid they're all right, Fitz," Ritchie said. "This doesn't mean anything. Did you find anything else? Like a tablet or diary or something?"

"Just a lot of clothes," Sokolov said. "And jewelry."

"Nothing covered with blood," Fitz said, then sighed. "That's really the thing that's going to prove it, isn't it? Whoever did this must've been covered in blood. And how would they get rid of that evidence?"

"Yeah, replicators won't recycle clothing covered in that much blood without flagging security," Wyss mumbled as if speaking only to himself. "Of course, the problem is we know our suspect can manipulate security programs with a scary level of skill. Maybe they could convince one to recycle the evidence without flagging anyone. That seems likely."

"And there's always good old-fashioned fire," Fitz said. "I guess we're back at square one."

"I wished I had all my drones here," Wyss said. "I could program them to search for blood traces and send them over the entire building and the whole local area. Frankly, I could start at the cottage and see if there's a trail to follow from there."

"Can't you just build more?" Ritchie asked. "There must be everything here you'd need to do that. We're on a central core planet."

"It would take time," Wyss said. "Like a week, at least."

"How come the security team here doesn't have drones that can do it?" Sokolov asked.

"What makes you think they don't?" a voice asked from the doorway. They all jumped guiltily, then turned to see Fitz's father in the doorway.

And right behind him, Lieutenant Klemm.

"Father," Fitz started to say, but his father silenced him with a single raised hand. He crossed the room to examine the pile of weapons on the floor. "I can explain," Fitz tried again to speak, but his father just raised that hand again, cutting him off.

"It's just as I told you, isn't it, sir?" Klemm said, and the general nodded.

Ritchie felt her stomach tie itself into a knot and then plunge down towards the ground fourteen floors below. What could Klemm possibly mean by that?

"It would appear so, lieutenant," Fitz's father said with great disappointment in his voice.

Ritchie hugged herself again, even though she was well away from the touch of the evening air.

"Father, I demand to know what he's accusing me of," Fitz said.

"You demand?" his father repeated, eyes narrowing.

"I have a right to know what I'm being accused of. Sir," Fitz said, not backing down.

He was doing that thing again, where he nudged his body between Ritchie and whatever he perceived to be danger. But this time, she let him. Because what if his father was here to take her away? Just him and Klemm? To finish what was started years before?

All her brain could summon up to say was, *why, why, why*?

"We brought these in from one of the guest rooms," Fitz said. "Is that really considered stealing?"

"No one has accused you of stealing," Klemm said coldly.

"What have I been accused of? And by whom?" Fitz said again.

"This has gone far beyond your usual childish nonsense, son," his father said. But he just turned away from all of them, slowly shaking his head.

"I'm not accusing you of anything, cadet," Klemm said.

"Then what's going on here?" Fitz demanded.

Klemm sighed, as if dealing with cadets was the most trying part of his day. He motioned for Fitz to step aside, but he stood his ground. So Klemm took a step to his left until he was able to see Ritchie once more. There was a vicious kind of triumph in his eyes as he pointed at her and said, "I accuse Cadet Ritchie of violating the terms of her parole."

"What?" they all cried out at once.

"I was here the entire time," Ritchie said. "I never left this room. I didn't use my implant. I did nothing I wasn't supposed to."

"The entire time," Fitz's father repeated from where he was pacing on the far side of the sofas. "The entire time of what?"

Ritchie opened her mouth, then shut it again. It was too late to take back those words.

"The entire time the rest of us were down on the tenth floor poking around in the guest rooms," Fitz said. "Against the rules, I know. So punish me. But Ritchie never left this room."

"Fitz," Ritchie said softly. There had to be a way out of this that didn't involve the rest of them getting into trouble, but trust Fitz not to find it. Sometimes she thought he thrived on getting caught, getting punished.

Well, of course he did. Because he had never been caught for lying to her. He had never been punished for that. So he just kept doing it to himself.

Ritchie put a hand to her forehead as if she could keep her mind from exploding. She must've made some sort of noise because Fitz spun around to look at her with great concern.

It was overwhelming. It was all too overwhelming.

But then Klemm raised a single finger and pointed it at Wyss. "And I accuse this one of doing the actual hacking of her implant. He changed the parole parameters and also spoofed her implant inputs to make us see what he wanted us to see."

Fitz spun back around to spit out an angry, "us?!?"

Ritchie wanted to speak in Wyss's defense, but she couldn't summon the words.

But Wyss didn't need her help. He looked calmly at Klemm and said, "there is no proof of that happening because it never happened. Have a tech come up and check her implant now. I never touched it."

"Ah, but we know that you did," Klemm said. "And furthermore…" he crossed the room to the far wall where the large display screen hung. He touched it, summoning it to life.

And gave Ritchie the oddest sensation she had ever experienced.

Because she was seeing the world through her own eyes. Through her own eyeballs. From just about an hour before.

They all stood there numbly, watching and listening as they had the same discussion as before, about searching the Schors' room.

How Fitz pressed for Ritchie to go with them. How Wyss said he could make it happen.

Only the moments where she refused to go were gone. Seamlessly.

Wyss watched it all, his normally pale face going a darker and darker shade of red. But when it ended, his voice was surprisingly calm as he said, "I can prove this is all fake. I can prove it."

"Of course you can," Klemm said, not quite smiling at all of them. "You're *clever*."

"Something very wrong is going on here," Fitz said, shaking his head. "Father, this isn't true. Ritchie never left this room. Have security check the feeds."

"They have, Fitz," his father said. He had stopped pacing, but now he stood so far across the room it was impossible to see what was going on with his facial expression. He sounded calm, but he often did. Just before the anger came.

Ritchie straightened her posture, forced her arms to stop hugging herself, and raised her chin as much as she could. Then, carefully keeping her voice steady, she asked, "What happens now?"

"Now you're all under house arrest," Klemm said.

"Paroles all around?" Fitz asked sarcastically.

"No, son," his father said from the far side of the room. "We've seen how little good that does against the likes of Cadet Wyss here."

"Then what?" Fitz asked.

He sounded scared. Fitz, scared, in his own house. Of his own father. Ritchie didn't know what to make of that.

"Human guards," Klemm said. "You'll be watched, physically watched, by guardians on a rotation. You will be confined to your rooms. Meals will be brought to you. You will not be leaving your rooms."

"Until when?" Fitz demanded.

Klemm just looked at him, that not-quite-a-smile never leaving his face.

Ritchie realized she was hugging herself again, but she left her arms where they were as she crossed the room to stand directly in front of Fitz's father. Klemm was behind her, far behind her, caught in a stare-down with Fitz.

"Until when, sir?" she asked him softly.

There it was again, that maddening look. But he just said, "until the real murderer is caught."

"And how is that going?" she asked.

Fitz's father sucked his teeth, then heaved out a sigh. "They tell me with every passing hour the odds of resolving this go down. Exponentially."

"It's been nearly twenty-four hours," Ritchie pointed out.

"That's correct," he said.

"And they're no closer?" she asked.

He raised an eyebrow at her. "You mean no closer than you are?"

Ritchie blinked at him. Was that some kind of joke?

But before she could ask, her old friend Guardian Rodin was there, hand gripping Ritchie's elbow far too tightly. Fitz's father watched Ritchie being dragged away, and Ritchie watched that inexplicable look on his face harden once more into stony anger.

The last thing she saw was Klemm left standing face to face with Fitz.

The look of triumph in the lieutenant's eyes was chillier than the night air.

16

FITZ SAT PRIMLY in the over-sized chair that desperately tried to suck him in, pull him down into a sullen slouch, swallow him up. He refused to let it, but it was awkward, sitting there almost at attention.

Completely ignored.

He had expected to be left in his room under guard, like his friends were, but somehow he had ended up here, back in his father's ridiculously over-sized and stone-cold office, sitting quietly while his father and Klemm worked.

He thought at first he was being dragged downstairs to be officially reprimanded by the general before being personally reprimanded by his father. The office was the perfect place for both of those things. Best-case scenario, he was finally going to be allowed to plead his case. He had his arguments at the ready.

But after being ordered to sit down, it was like he had turned invisible. Or worse, ceased to exist. Why was he even there? It wasn't like his father didn't have better things to do than babysit him personally.

Hoping that pleading his case was still an option if he was patient, Fitz tried to wait the two of them out.

But it wasn't easy. The musty smell of the books around him was already coating the back of his throat, but it was the dustiness of the pages that was taunting him with a tickling cough he didn't dare give in to.

"There's that taken care of," his father said, handing a tablet to Klemm then tapping at something on his desktop. "What's next?"

"The diplomat position must be filled again, as soon as possible, sir," Klemm said, juggling a stack of tablets before setting one in front of the general.

Fitz watched his father scroll down a list on that tablet, then set it aside with a look of disgust. "No. I ruled all of these people out the first time around. I'm not going through them again."

"They are the only qualified applicants, sir," Klemm said with infinite patience. "You'll have to pick one of them. I'm sure you can make it work with any of them, given enough time."

"Time that we don't have," his father grumbled, but picked the tablet up again all the same.

"I would like to point to Diplomat Karre again, sir," Klemm said. "I do believe he is the best of that batch."

"Yes, you said so before," Fitz's father said as he tugged at his bottom lip. "I disagreed, as you recall. Lavatar was perfect."

Klemm said nothing. Fitz sensed that Klemm had always advocated for this Karre fellow over Lavatar, and was trying to do so again. But delicately.

"Sir, should I at least schedule a personal interview for you and Diplomat Karre?" Klemm asked when the silence had stretched out too long.

Fitz's father made a noncommittal sound, still studying the tablet. Then he looked up at Klemm. "These are the only qualified applicants, correct? That's what you said?"

"Correct, sir," Klemm said.

"So these are the diplomats who *applied*?" the general pressed.

"Sir?"

"There might be other qualified diplomats who didn't apply?"

"Recent graduates, you mean?" Klemm asked.

"Or who were satisfied with their positions the last time we put out the call, but might not be so this time. Or who might need a personal meeting from me to convince them to take the job," Fitz's father said.

Klemm sighed. "Sir, I remind you that this position simply must be filled as soon as possible."

"Yes, you've said," the general said. There was the tiniest of edges to his voice. Klemm's face showed no reaction, but all the hairs on the back of Fitz's neck were standing on end. He could feel that storm of anger coming. "The position must be filled as soon as possible, and Diplomat Karre is the best fit. That's what you're saying?"

"Yes, sir," Klemm said.

Fitz's father nodded, looking down at the tablet again. Then he abruptly thrust it into Klemm's already full arms. Klemm struggled to grasp it as well as the others he was already holding. For a second, Fitz braced for the sound of maximum confidentiality tablets raining down on the stone floor. But Klemm managed to get them all stacked neatly in his arms once more.

"Go to the secure communications room and arrange the meeting," Fitz's father said, and, as if dismissing Klemm from his mind entirely, he focused on his open desktop.

"Sir, I can have Lieutenant Gore handle that," Klemm said.

"No, I want you to do it personally, Lieutenant," Fitz's father said without looking up.

Fitz fought the urge to grin as he watched Klemm war with himself. He must want this Karre fellow in the diplomat post pretty badly for it to conflict so strongly with his ever-present drive to never leave the general's side.

Then those dark eyes fixed on Fitz. Fitz, who had started to think he was invisible.

"Sir, Diplomat Karre is on Jorda at the moment. It would be the middle of the night in the capital now. I will see to it personally, of course, but it would be best to wait a few hours, I think."

Fitz's father tapped at the edge of his desktop with the side of his stylus as if lost in thought. "So as soon as possible has been downgraded to as soon as it's convenient, Lieutenant?" he asked.

"No, sir," Klemm said. Then he was looking at Fitz again.

"If you'd rather I go, I'd be happy to accommodate you," Fitz said.

"No, you're staying where you are," his father said before Klemm could say a word.

"Why? So I can explain myself? I'd be happy to do that now, and then I can go and you can get on with… whatever," Fitz said, gesturing at Klemm's stack of tablets and his father's desktop both.

"I can summon a guardian to escort him back to his room, sir," Klemm offered.

"I don't need you to do that, lieutenant. I need you to follow my first order and contact this Diplomat Karre. Is there any particular reason you're still here?" he asked, fixing his aide-de-camp with a withering stare that would have Fitz scuttling off to do anything at all as quickly as he could.

But Klemm was impervious to that stare, apparently. "I can have Lieutenant Gore get him on the line for you to speak with directly, sir. If you want him rousted out of bed to hear your offer, sir."

"Him and Gore both," Fitz's father grumbled. His eyes darted up and to the side, the classic gesture of someone checking their implant's chronometer. Fitz immediately checked his own. Well past midnight.

"Is there a reason I'm still here?" Fitz asked. "It's late, and I'm tired. If I'm going to sleep here under your watchful eye, can I at least get a cot?"

He didn't cherish the thought of trying to sleep in this cold, damp, cavernous space, but he doubted it would come to that.

But was the plan to make him bunk down in his parents' room? Put a cot in the corner, or at the foot of their bed? That wasn't much better.

But neither of the two officers even seemed to hear him.

"Lieutenant Gore bunks on the fourth floor, correct?" his father asked Klemm.

"Yes, sir," Klemm said, sounding relieved. "I'll send a runner to go wake him." He started towards the door. The moment his back was turned, Fitz's father dropped his head, gripping at his own hair in a gesture of frustration that Fitz knew quite well. He did it himself all the time.

"No, Lieutenant," the general said, raising his head before Klemm turned back to give him a questioning look. "No, let him sleep. I'll call Diplomat Karre myself in a few hours, when it's dawn in the capital on Jorda."

"Very good, sir," Klemm said.

"In the meantime, I'd like to walk my son up to his bedroom," he said.

"Of course, sir. I'll just put these tablets back in the vault and join you," Klemm said.

He ducked behind a bookcase that Fitz hadn't even realized was a doorway. But that wasn't the most startling thing going on in that room.

If Fitz didn't know better, he'd think his father was struggling with feelings of great powerlessness. His father, the general and the governor of the planet they were standing on. How could he possibly be powerless?

And yet Fitz could feel the frustration coming off him in waves.

"What's going on here, father?" Fitz hissed. But his father just shook his head at him with a sharp look of warning. Then Klemm was back. How did that man move so quickly?

"All set. Shall we?" Klemm said to the two of them.

"Sir," Fitz said. Then lifted his eyebrows when Klemm just looked at him in confusion. "'Shall we, *sir*?' That's what you meant to say, right? Because the last time I checked, a general still outranks a lieutenant."

Klemm just stood there, slowly blinking four times. Then he said, "of course. You are quite correct, cadet. But I was addressing you specifically. No reason for your father to go out of his way on your account when I'm perfectly capable of walking you back to your room. The general needs his sleep."

"Is that true? Does the general need his sleep?" Fitz asked his father.

"Don't be impertinent, Fitz," his father said. But ironically, he did sound quite tired.

"Sorry, father," Fitz said. "But if your desktop is still online, perhaps you can open up your agenda for tomorrow and find five minutes to talk to me? You brought me all the way here from Oymyakon, after all. I'm missing classes for this, whatever *this* is."

"I schedule all the general's appointments, cadet," Klemm said. "I shall take a look first thing in the morning, but I'm afraid it's rather unlikely I will find even five minutes for you. The murder investigation has really thrown a wrench into things. I'm sure you understand."

"Seriously?" Fitz asked. But his father wasn't meeting his eyes. Fitz just threw his hands in the air in frustration. "Whatever. I'm too tired for this. Come, Lieutenant Klemm. To bed!"

There was some small satisfaction in the fact that his father didn't chide his impertinence that time. But only a small amount.

Mostly, as Fitz walked with Klemm beside him back to his bedroom, he longed to go straight to Ritchie and talk all of this over with her in detail. She was watching Klemm and his father, too. What were her impressions?

Because all Fitz knew was that it was nuts. Which was far from a helpful takeaway.

But Ritchie was under guard in her room with Moreau, just like he was about to be under guard in his own room. Getting five minutes alone with her was now as impossible as getting five minutes alone with his father had been since he arrived.

Fitz had never felt so isolated in his life.

17

RITCHIE HAD LAIN FULLY DRESSED on top of her bed, not even pretending to sleep, for hours in the dark before another guardian had finally arrived to relieve Guardian Rodin.

Rodin, with her accusing eyes. How was Ritchie supposed to sleep with that woman glaring judgment at her nonstop?

Not that Moreau was having any problem. The soft sounds of her snoring blended with the rustling of the curtains and the drone of the nighttime insects below.

Ritchie watched Rodin slip out of the room. Then she saw the new guardian looking down at her.

"Still awake?" the woman whispered. Ritchie nodded. "Do you need something to sleep?"

"You mean like a drug?" Ritchie whispered back.

"If you like. But I was thinking more of a warm glass of milk. Always does the trick for me," the guardian said.

"No, but is it all right if I go out on the balcony for a few minutes? The wind blowing the grass in the moonlight is kind of calming for me," Ritchie said, desperately hoping that she didn't sound too eager.

"Hypnotic, isn't it? Sure, go ahead," the guardian said. Then she turned to adjust the chair Rodin had been sitting in, angling it more towards the door to the hallway than the two beds or the open balcony doors beyond.

Ritchie slipped outside and went to stand at the railing, resting her elbows on the edge as she looked down at the grasslands below.

This guardian seemed nice, willing to give them a measure of privacy. Not that Ritchie thought she could sneak away. Even through the gauzy curtains, she could tell from the guardian's posture that she was alert and watchful. She was doing her job faithfully, but she wasn't going to be unduly harsh about it.

Unlike Rodin, who had taken a sneering delight in Ritchie's inability to sleep while that woman glared down at her.

It irked her a lot. How much she was being forced to hope that Rodin was actually good at her job. Because Rodin and Wahli were clearly in charge of the investigation. The faster they found a real suspect, the faster Ritchie's life could go back to normal.

Whatever that meant now.

But were they even running a proper investigation? She had seen signs of meticulous evidence collection, sure, but was anyone processing that evidence with any degree of attention? Or were they just so convinced that Ritchie was their suspect that they had stopped looking for anything besides evidence to convict her?

They all answered to Fitz's father, after all. And the one thing that Fitz's father had always done when it came to Ritchie was try to remove her from Fitz's vicinity. He had succeeded at that for a long time, but that time was over now. Was he feeling frustration at that fact?

How far was he willing to go to keep them apart?

Was this entire trip not about Fitz's parole on Braga at all? Was it always about getting Ritchie here, under his power, where he could do whatever he wanted with her? Pin anything at all on her?

Because she had decided to go to guardian school. Which meant she would stay close to Fitz for another four years. Someone who wanted them apart would surely have a huge problem with that.

Ritchie chewed at her lip. That all sounded like sound logic to her. Except for the look she kept seeing in the general's eyes.

She wished she knew if he knew that she knew everything. Or that it was possible to just have that conversation out loud and be done with it.

She, the general, and Fitz in a room with no Klemm in it. She dreaded that confrontation with all her being, but she knew it was necessary. Would everything be rosy after all those words were said? No way. But it had to be better.

It couldn't be worse.

She hunched over the balcony railing, resting her chin on her hands. The tranquility of the view just wasn't doing it for her. It didn't lend her any amount of peace. And it hadn't the night before either.

"I could probably hop that wall again," Fitz whispered, almost making her jump out of her skin. She had been focusing so intently on the grass below and the turmoil of her own thoughts that she hadn't even realized he was there beside her, on his own balcony. The wall was between them, but they were so close their elbows were nearly touching.

"Don't do it," Ritchie hissed back at him. "I have a guardian who could look out here at any moment."

"Me, too," Fitz whispered. "I told mine I needed a breath of fresh air, but really, I just hoped you'd be out here. And here you are." She could tell even as he kept his voice as quiet as he could that he was nervous. Tentative. Not sure what response she was going to give him.

But she didn't have any anger left in her. Just fear.

"I can't sleep," she said.

"That's hardly surprising. Is it okay if I stand here with you?" he asked.

"Why wouldn't it be?" she asked.

"Come on. You've been mad at me all day," he said.

"I'm not mad at you," she said.

"More fool me, then," he said with a shrug.

"I was a little bit mad at you," she admitted. "You waited a long time to unload all that on me."

"Are you kidding? I still told you too soon. I really wanted to talk to my father first."

"And have you? Talked to your father?" she asked.

"Not properly. Lieutenant Klemm won't allow it," he said.

"He won't allow it?" Ritchie asked. And yet, that was how it felt to her, too. "What do we know about Klemm?"

"Only what Wyss told us," Fitz said with another shrug. "That doesn't feel like the whole story, does it?" he went on. "But I just can't figure out what's really going on. I would almost think he's steering my father around, if that wasn't basically unthinkable."

"He's only worked for your father for a few years, right?" Ritchie asked.

"Months," Fitz said.

"So your father keeping me out of the foreign service academies was before his time?"

"Yeah," Fitz said. "I think that was to protect you, not punish you. For what that's worth."

"I think it was to protect *you*," Ritchie said.

"Possibly," Fitz conceded. Ritchie hated that she couldn't see his face. There was just a silvery outline of his chin, his nose, of that lock of hair that always fell over his forehead. Nothing that would give her a hint to what he was thinking.

"I was thinking, maybe that's why I'm here now," she said.

"What do you mean?" Fitz asked.

"Maybe I'm here so that your father can make sure that you are protected," she said, really hoping that she didn't have to spell it all out.

"That makes no sense. You're here because I invited you. I didn't tell him until we were boarding the shuttle. That way, he couldn't say no."

"He could've refused to let me on board," Ritchie pointed out.

"So you think I invited you because he manipulated me, too?" Fitz said, then shook his head. "No, I brought you here because I wanted to tell you what I told you last night. And there's no way he wanted that."

"Then he let me come because he saw an opportunity," Ritchie said.

"For what?" Fitz asked. Almost too loudly, she gestured for him to keep his voice down. He repeated, but more lowly this time, "for what?"

"To get rid of me before you get stuck spending four more years in my company," she said.

"What are you talking about?" he asked. He truly sounded confused, almost miserably so.

"You and I both know I'm being framed here. And the investigators aren't working very hard to find any other suspects."

"They've held up a large number of important people," Fitz reminded her.

"What better way to sell the story?" Ritchie said.

"You think my father is framing you for murder just to keep you out of guardian school?" he asked, his skepticism clear.

"It's not inconceivable," she said.

"Well, so what if he is? We're not going to let him get away with that," he said, borderline too loudly again. But Ritchie was finding it harder to care. So what if they were caught talking? What was the worse that would happen? They'd put her in one of the cells down in the basement? She had lived through worse.

"Maybe we should," she found herself saying. "Maybe that would be easier."

"Oh, sure. Because when people think of Cadet Ritchie, they think of someone always taking the easier path," he said sarcastically.

"I'm serious," she said.

"You want to be framed for murder? You're going to take that lying down?" he asked.

"No, that's not what I meant," she said.

"So, what did you mean? Give up on guardian school? No way."

"Why not?"

"Because getting out of a fake murder charge is no reason to go to that cold-ass diplomat school," he hissed at her.

"I wasn't even thinking of diplomat school," she said, a touch more defensively than she had intended.

"What are you saying? You want to get out of foreign service entirely?" he asked.

"Why not? I have many talents. I could acquire any of a variety of skills. I could go to any school, pretty much, and work hard enough to do well. I know that in my bones," she said.

Fitz was quiet for a long time. It was like the crickets below grew louder to fill in that silence. Then he finally said, so low she could barely hear him, "you're thinking of business school, then? With Guy Travert?"

That startled her. She hadn't been thinking of Guy at all. "No."

"Well, what then?" he asked, but didn't wait for her to answer. "No, whatever you're thinking, I'm going to say no. I'm going to say no to anything that means you're not in guardian school next year. Sorry, but that's the only acceptable outcome, Ritchie."

"So I don't get a say?" she shot back.

"Not when you're talking crazy," he said.

"Is it crazy? Really? That I do something else? Anything else?"

"Yes," he said. Then even the silhouette of his face was gone from the light. It took her half a second to realize this was because he had turned to face her. She had both moons full on her face. He could see her perfectly clearly. But all she could make out was the shape of his hair.

Then his hands were on hers, holding her tightly, as if afraid she was going to fall over the side. But she was nowhere near the balcony.

"Fitz?" she asked, a little unnerved by this sudden intense energy from him.

"You're staying with me, Ritchie. End of discussion."

"You don't get to decide that, Fitz," she said. But she couldn't bring herself to pull her hands away from his. Why was that?

"You can't leave me. Not now."

"You act like everything is already mended between us when it isn't," she said. Although in truth, her anger was all gone now. He had messed things up, keeping secrets and putting up walls. He had messed things up a lot.

But if she was honest with herself, she didn't know what she could have done better if their positions had been reversed. Like, totally reversed. If Fitz's father was her father. Because Fitz's father loomed larger than life.

Would she have had the courage to cross him even as much as Fitz had?

But Fitz sounded contrite when she said, "I know. I know. But we're at the beginning of that, right?"

"Maybe," she said.

"But it can't happen at all if we're not still together. Like, physically close to each other," he said, and squeezed her hands just a little tighter.

Her chest felt tight, because she knew he didn't mean what she was thinking. That earnestness in his eyes not to lose her, wasn't about the version of her standing on that balcony. Not really. It was about the twelve-year-old version of her he lost years ago. That's what he wanted back. That's what he could never risk losing.

But how could she get him to see her as she was now? Who she was now?

"It might be easier if we're not," she said. "What if we're not guardians together?"

"No," he said. It sounded like that word choked him on the way out. She felt a little bad. It was like she was crushing his dream. But she didn't see another way.

She gently pulled back on her right hand, freeing it from his grasp. Then she did the one thing she had wanted to do for so long. She reached up and brushed back that lock of his hair.

It was just as soft as she had imagined.

"Ritchie?" He sounded thoroughly confused.

"Look, there is still a lot to be sorted out between us. But I can think of one upside of not doing it when we're both guardians," she said. That lock of hair slipped from her fingers to fall over his forehead, and she just had to brush it back again.

"What?" he asked. Still choking. Still hating that idea. Still not getting what she was really saying.

"Can't you guess?" she said. But she knew he didn't. So she freed her other hand and pulled his head down until her lips could find his.

He made a muffled yelp of surprise, but only briefly. Then he was kissing her back.

And that, too, felt just as she had always imagined.

18

IT WAS like time had stopped. The light from the moons hung frozen all around them. The breeze that had been dancing through Ritchie's hair now held it suspended mid-tousle. Even the drone of the insects below had lost its rise and fall. It was one steady sound that went on forever.

At least Fitz decided that was what was going on. He had no other reason to be stuck in that moment, unable to summon a single thought let alone take an action. He was powerless.

Ritchie was kissing him. And all he could do was kiss her back.

But as amazing as that fact was, as amazing as everything about that moment was, it was tainted. Because he knew what was really going on.

Ritchie was giving up. On everything.

And there was no way he could let her do that.

The moonlight broke free first. Then he felt the coolness of the breeze on his cheek, such a sharp contrast to the heat from her hand now curved around the back of his neck. The insects sang all the louder, as if to make up for those lost seconds.

And Fitz finally found the strength of will to grab Ritchie by the shoulders and move her back away from him.

But not far enough. She made a little complaining noise and reached for him again, and he had to step back, well out of her reach, with the wall between them. She blinked, then flushed scarlet as if suddenly realizing what was happening. Even in the moonlight, he could see the pink of her cheeks.

"I thought," Ritchie started to say, but then broke off. Her shoulders slumped low, and misery radiated off from her in waves. "Never mind. I was wrong."

"Listen," Fitz said, but had no followup to that. He ran his hands through his hair, just like he always did when he was frustrated.

And Ritchie meeped.

Just like she had that one time in the cafeteria back on Oymyakon. And just now she had touched his hair with something almost like reverence.

But that would mean this wasn't a new thing? She had actually been attracted to him for quite some time? And he had had no clue?

It was too much to unpack. Every memory of every moment between them wanted to rush to the front of his brain for re-analysis, and there just wasn't the time.

And it wouldn't even matter, really. It didn't change his own feelings a bit. She was still giving up, and he still wasn't going to let her do that. Not even if it meant that he had to give up... whatever this had been about to lead to. Not even then. He couldn't let her do that, not even if it was somehow all for him.

No, especially not for him.

"Listen," he said again, then caught himself about to brush his hair back again. That felt really weird now. He dropped his hand. "We're not going to do this."

"Yeah, you made that really clear," Ritchie said.

"Not because I don't want to," he admitted.

"But?" she said, not looking at him.

"I'm not ready to concede defeat, especially not to my father," he said. "We're going to figure this all out. And then we're going to guardian school together. And in four years, whatever comes next, we're doing that too. But we both know that means that anything between us besides being friends is going to have to wait. For at least four years, maybe more."

"It's really that important to you?" Ritchie asked.

"You being a guardian? Absolutely," he said.

"I meant *you* being a guardian," she said.

He had guessed that. "I'm not doing it without you. If you quit or let my father drive you out or—worse—let yourself get framed for this murder, that's the end of it for me, too."

"It's entirely possible that after guardian school we get assigned to postings that aren't even on the same side of the Union of Free Worlds, let alone the same planet. We could be days and dozens of jump points apart, for years."

"I'm sure by the end of guardian school there won't be a soul in the Union of Free Worlds that wouldn't see that we belong together," he said. "We work well together. We fit. We always have. I don't want to try to recreate that with anyone else. Do you?"

Ritchie pondered this in silence for a long moment, then finally shook her head.

"Good. We agree," he said.

She sighed heavily. "This doesn't change my feelings about what you did."

"I know," he said. "But isn't that part of how we work? This isn't the first time we've had to set aside some pretty heavy baggage and work together anyway to solve a murder. We do that really well, don't we?"

"It seems that way," Ritchie conceded, but she still sounded irritated with him. "It's not great that we have to. A lot. But we *do* do it."

"So let's do that again now. Once this is over and we have the real murderer safely in custody, we can sit down and take all the time in the world to sort this out." He raked his hands through his hair again and sighed in frustration. "I lied to you for years. I know it. I hated it, but I did it. I thought I owed it to my father. But my father doesn't feel like he owes me even five minutes of his time," he said.

"Still?" Ritchie asked. "I think something is going on there with Klemm."

"Oh, something is definitely going on there with Klemm," he said. "It's just another thing that we have to deal with second, though."

"The murder," Ritchie said glumly. "We have no evidence except what leads back to me."

"And we learned nothing when we searched the Schors' room," Fitz said. "They're still suspects, but the more I think about it, the less they make sense."

"Because of the security systems at the diplomat cottage being hacked like that," Ritchie said. "Yes, I was thinking the same thing. I don't think either of them could do it. They might be able to hire someone to do it for them, but even that would leave evidence, the sort the investigators would have already."

"Or Wyss. He searched their digital footprints pretty thoroughly. If they had been in anything like suspicious-sounding contact with anyone, he would've seen it."

"And now we're all on house arrest, so no more mingling with the other guests," Ritchie said. "How are we going to find more suspects?"

"I don't know," Fitz said. Then he stepped closer to her so that he could sneak a peek inside her room. He could make out Moreau's sleeping form on the closer of the two beds. More dimly at the far side of the room, all but lost in the shadows, he saw the outline of the guardian. She was sitting in a chair turned towards the door. She could see the two of them standing there if she turned her head just a little bit to the right. But she never did.

"I don't think we're without allies," he whispered to Ritchie.

"No, but I'm not sure how we tell friend from foe," she whispered back.

"Maybe they'll make themselves known to us," he said, but that wasn't a hope he wanted to depend on.

"You need to see your father," Ritchie said.

"I know," he sighed.

"No, seriously. You need to find a way to get your father to meet you. Up here or in his office, whichever. We just need him tied up with you for a little bit of time."

"I don't know what you're planning, but you should know that Klemm never leaves his side," Fitz said.

"I know," she said, and she was grinning up at him.

"Wait, what's your plan?" he asked.

"If your father meets with you, and Klemm has to be there for whatever reasons he has for doing that, that leaves the rest of us free to search his room," she said.

"Could you even get in there? He has high security clearance. That means his office and personal chambers are both secured locations," Fitz said.

"Wyss can do it," she said.

Which was likely true. But… "How is Wyss going to know he needs to do it? He's in a room all on his own," Fitz said.

Her grin widened, and he felt his heart lift even though she had yet to tell him why he should feel more hopeful. He just knew. This was all going to be okay.

"You remember earlier in your sitting room, when Wyss noticed before I did that my parole had been modified?"

"To keep you out of the Schors' room, right," Fitz said.

"He knew that because he had been poking at my implant from his tablet," Ritchie said. "He didn't try hacking it. He was just probing it for weaknesses, I think."

"How do you know that? You haven't had a moment alone with Wyss since?" Fitz said, frowning.

"He told me," she said. Then she tapped her forehead.

"What's that mean?" Fitz asked.

"He didn't hack my implant or touch my parole, but he did insert just a little bit of code. Enough for him to get messages through to me. They display on my chronometer. Six characters at a time. It's a little hard to follow, but I know he's in contact and waiting for orders, basically."

"But how can you contact him in return?" Fitz asked.

"I set my alarm," Ritchie said. "Six characters at a time. They don't even have to be numbers, although letters generate an error code I have to clear every time. It's tedious, but doable."

"And no one knows you're doing this?"

"It doesn't trigger any notifications. If someone checked my time or alarm settings, they would see that they make no sense, and that they keep changing. But why would anyone bother with that? Seeing through my eyes without consent is so much cooler." She rolled her eyes, but he just felt another grin coming on. Her attitude was so much better than even five minutes ago.

"You're talking to him now?" he guessed.

"Slowly. And actually I should go inside because I think this would be easier if I weren't talking to you at the same time."

"Sure," Fitz said. "So I'll demand to see my father in the morning, and then I'll keep him and Klemm occupied while the rest of you...?"

"Hack our implants, hack his security measures, and rifle through his stuff," Ritchie said. "That's pretty much it."

"I hope it works," he said. "Although it is checking off the to-do list out of order."

"Klemm might know more than we do about what happened to Diplomat Lavatar," Ritchie said. "But even if we just find out why he acts the way he does, maybe we can find a way to remove him from the board, so to speak. Solving the murder will be easier with him no longer interfering. Arresting me and then putting us all under house arrest both felt like Klemm's ideas, not your father's."

"Agreed. And can I just say, I like this plan?"

"Thanks. Me, too," she said, grinning.

They were standing close again, only the wall between them, and his hands were on her shoulders as she gazed up at him. He realized almost too late that he was about to kiss her again and quickly steered away, planting a fond kiss on her forehead instead. Then he stepped away from her.

"Good night, Ritchie," he said.

"Good night, Fitz," she said. He watched her slip back into her room. As if in sympathy, the two moons slid behind the clouds, and it was too dark to see more.

Fitz went back to his bed, knowing full well he would sleep even less than he had the night before.

19

RITCHIE WOKE UP, which was a little disorienting. She hadn't expected to sleep at all, and didn't remember drifting off. She had, in fact, been in the process of messaging with Wyss. She must've fallen asleep while waiting for his response.

Now it was midmorning, the sun shining hotly through the open windows. But she could still smell breakfast. Coffee and eggs. And bacon. She was pretty sure it was the smell of bacon that had pulled her from sleep. She certainly didn't feel like she had rested enough.

"Good morning," Moreau said when Ritchie had sat up to look blearily around the room. "Guardian Rodin is here with us again, but she brought breakfast."

"Breakfast sounds good," Ritchie said. Which was more than she could say for the first part of the message. She had never even caught the other guardian's name. But she knew that woman had let her and Fitz talk as long as they wanted the night before. She owed her thanks for that.

"After breakfast, we just sit here," Moreau said as she thrust a plate of eggs and bacon with toast into Ritchie's hands. "Apparently, lunch isn't guaranteed to happen. A lot is going on downstairs, we have to understand. Dinner will be room service again, followed by more sitting around until bedtime."

"You know, cadet, your tone isn't going unnoticed," Guardian Rodin said from her chair near the door. It was once more positioned to face the two beds and the balcony beyond, so she could observe Moreau and Ritchie as closely as she wanted to.

And she clearly wanted to do it very closely indeed.

"Tone?" Moreau said, blinking innocently as she sat down on her own bed and picked up her coffee mug to take a delicate sip.

"You know what I mean, cadet. And I'll be sure to notate it on my report," Rodin said. Moreau raised her eyebrows in mock-shock but said nothing.

"I have to go to the bathroom," Ritchie said, setting her plate on the nightstand.

"Go ahead, cadet," Rodin said. Not that Ritchie had been asking permission. Ritchie went inside the other room and closed the door. Through it, she could still hear the muffled voice of Rodin. "I can hear what's going on in there, and I'm keeping my eye on the clock, so no funny business."

It wasn't the main reason she had come in here, but Ritchie went about her morning routine, anyway. It would keep her on Rodin's clock, and she could do it on autopilot.

Because Wyss had somehow known the instant she was awake and had started sending messages to her through her chronometer. She had gotten better at reading them, six characters at a time, and keeping it all in her head until it started to make sense. But sending a response required a lot more focus. A level of focus that would make it hard to keep up with Moreau's conversation. She might just seem like she was sleep-deprived or generally spacy, but she was afraid it was the sort of thing that Rodin would notice. And question.

Klemm, or perhaps Fitz's father, seemed to think Wyss was the biggest risk, so he had two guardians in his room. And no privacy, even in his bathroom. The very idea was kind of horrific, but Wyss just shrugged it off.

They weren't wrong to distrust him. Because apparently he had for years tinkered with his own implant. He preferred working on tablets with screens, but he never needed to. All he needed to do was close his eyes and his implant could do anything. And he could see it all in his field of view. He could communicate with Ritchie, hack into the security systems, finish his homework back on Oymyakon, whatever he wanted, really. And he could do it all at once.

And to the two guardians who were watching him, it just looked like he was napping. Again. Because that's what teenaged boys did best.

So he had assured Ritchie many times that while it was impossible for him to leave his room at all, it was also completely unnecessary. Whatever they needed from him, he could do it and never raise a bit of suspicion.

Ritchie also got the sense that he had been up all night, even after she had dropped off to sleep. He had a thorough knowledge of the building, the locations of everything, and exactly how the security systems functioned. He had everything worked out, except for how to get any of them out of their rooms in the first place.

Ritchie wasn't above teaming up with Moreau to take Rodin out, but she didn't want that to be Plan A. Firstly, it might not even work. She hadn't seen Rodin in a fight, but she was built like a kickboxer. Ritchie didn't like her chances, even with Moreau on her side. They'd have to try hitting her from behind, which was all but impossible when she always sat with her back to the wall.

So that was her and Moreau out, in addition to Wyss.

And Fitz was needed as their diversion. Even if they could break him out, it wouldn't help.

Which left only Sokolov.

That was where she and Wyss had left things the night before. Now he was messaging her with a plan to reach Sokolov through her implant. He couldn't do it the same way he had reached Ritchie, since he had piggy-backed on her parole to access her implant. But he had another plan he thought might work.

If it did, the rest would be much easier. Because Sokolov was the opposite of Wyss. They thought so little of any risk she might represent that they had a single rookie guardian watching her. And that rookie had been reprimanded four times since coming to Buennagel, basically for chatting while she should be on duty. If Sokolov could slip past her or just take her out, it would be easy enough for Wyss to guide her to Klemm's rooms.

"Taking a lot of time, cadet," Rodin said through the door. Ritchie sighed and ran her hands through her hair. Then on impulse she started running a fingertip over the mirror, scrawling a hasty message on the glass. She had just finished when the door she knew she had locked burst open and Rodin stood there glaring at her.

"I was coming out," Ritchie said, still standing at the sink and drying her hands on a towel.

"Your breakfast is getting cold," Rodin said, then gestured for her to go back out to the bedroom.

"Hey," Moreau said blandly as Ritchie sat back down on her bed and turned her attention back to her indeed cold breakfast.

"Hey," Ritchie said, matching Moreau's tone. "I know we have all day, but after I'm done with this food, I wanted to hit the shower."

"Okay?" Moreau said, clearly aware that she was missing some-thing important but unable to ask what it was.

"I mean, I know you like to take long showers, so if you want to get in there first, maybe do it now?" Ritchie said, and stuffed a forkful of eggs in her mouth.

"I do like showers," Moreau said, not quite uplifting the end of that sentence to turn it into a question, but almost.

"Long, hot, *steamy* showers," Ritchie said, and ate another mouthful of eggs.

"Well, now you've totally put me in the mood," Moreau said, setting her coffee mug aside. "Guardian Rodin, permission to use the shower?"

"Get in there," Rodin said impatiently. "I'm watching the clock."

"Of course," Moreau said, then disappeared into the bathroom. Ritchie munched on her bacon. The steam from the shower would coat the mirror, everywhere except where the oils from her fingertip had marred the glass. She hadn't been able to fit much on that square of space, but it was enough to let Moreau know there was a plan and it was moving along nicely.

Then Wyss was back in her chronometer, letting her know that Sokolov had indeed opened the message that seemed to come from

Oymyakon and contain her assignments for that week's history class that she was missing. She had sent back a templated received response as a signal. That would only look weird if whoever was watching her implant activity knew that Sokolov never sent templated responses. She liked to keep things personable and human.

Meanwhile, Wyss was still working on a side project. Ritchie rolled her eyes as she put the last of her eggs on one of the slices of toast and folded the bread over it before biting into it. Of course, Wyss had a side project. Why do just ten things at once when you could do twenty?

As she chewed, the message continued, bit by bit, in her chronometer display. He was working on a way to create a private secured space where they could all communicate through their implants without anyone else knowing. They could all talk to each other through the texting feature, and unless they reacted to it, no one around them would ever know.

As much as Ritchie had grown to hate her implant over the last few years, she had to admit that hacking it to make it something more under her control felt pretty good.

She got up from her bed to put her empty plate on the tray set in front of the door. But a sudden thought came to her, and she turned to Rodin. "So, if you're here, who is working the investigation? I thought that was under your and Wahli's command."

"I'm not going to be here all day," Rodin told her, bending over to adjust the placement of Ritchie's plate. As if she had somehow set it down wrong.

"Still, no more leads?" Ritchie asked.

"Not that I'm sharing with you," Rodin said.

"Can you at least tell me if Fitz got to talk with his father?" Ritchie asked.

"That's even less my business than it is yours," Rodin said. But she relented a little and added, "although I doubt it. The general is currently off planet."

"What?" Ritchie gasped. "How could he leave now, with all that's going on?"

"He's not personally conducting the investigation. He has greater responsibilities," Rodin said. "I wouldn't think that would be a hard concept for you to grasp."

"Off planet, to where?" Ritchie asked.

"None of our business," Rodin said sharply.

"How far away? When will he be back?" Ritchie pressed.

"Honestly, cadet. I shouldn't have to explain this to you," Rodin said. Then the bathroom door clicked open and Moreau emerged from a thick cloud of steam. Rodin waved the vapor away from her face, annoyed. "I guess you do like your showers steamy, don't you?"

"You have no idea how much better I feel," Moreau said, then winked at Ritchie the moment her back was to Rodin before heading to where she had left her bag to find her brush.

Another message for Wyss started coming through, almost faster than she could manage. Ritchie lay back on her bed and threw an arm over her eyes, blocking out the room around her to focus just on the text on her chronometer display. She vaguely heard Moreau and Rodin saying something about rest and headaches, but she deliberately steered her attention away.

Sokolov was out of her room. More, she had reached Klemm's personal rooms. She had found something, but there were guardians outside the apartment now and she couldn't get out again.

The last bit of Wyss' message was a question. *Permission to start a ruckus?*

Ritchie bit her lip hard to keep from grinning.

"Maybe you should get her something?" Moreau said to Rodin.

"I'm not leaving this room, cadet," Rodin growled back.

Ritchie laboriously typed out her reply in her alarm-setting function. *Absolutely.*

Ritchie wondered what the ruckus would be. She half-expected to hear alarms sounding all over the building, maybe people running around in barely contained panic.

But in the end, all that happened was that Rodin sat up a little straighter on her chair.

Then she said, "I have to go. I'm locking you in."

Moreau started to object, but Rodin was gone in a flash, leaving nothing behind but the very final-sounding click of the bolt sliding home.

"What was that about?" Moreau asked.

"Wyss had to make a ruckus to get Sokolov out of Klemm's office," Ritchie told her. "I'm sure it's in no way coincidental that all guardian hands are needed on deck to deal with the ruckus."

"Nice," Moreau said. "So what do we do?"

"For now, we wait," Ritchie said. "Wyss will have us all linked through our implants soon enough."

"*Did* Fitz get to talk to his father?" Moreau asked.

"I don't think so," Ritchie sighed. "But Sokolov found something. I really hope it's something useful."

"We need a break in this case, that's for sure," Moreau said.

"We need to get rid of Klemm," Ritchie said. "Everything will be easier without him here."

But maybe that wasn't even true. Because he wasn't there now. He was off-planet with Fitz's father. And nothing else had changed.

She wondered, if he had woken to find his father no longer on Buennagel, just what Fitz was doing now.

20

FITZ STOOD inside the doorway of his mother's dance studio, almost overwhelmed by the rush of memories that were triggered by that space. It was easily the size of the formal dining room far below it, but the lack of furniture within made it feel larger. All the glass doors along the north-facing wall were opened up onto the balcony, but the sheer curtains were pulled closed to filter out the harshest of the light. They were on the fifth floor, close enough to the grasslands for the smell of the Immerweis to be strongly present. It mingled pleasantly with the lemony smell of whatever was used to maintain the wooden floorboards to a glassy sheen. It looked like it was coated in mirrors, but it clung ever so slightly to the bottoms of his feet, like he was standing in something sticky.

How many hours had he spent here as a young child, watching his mother rehearse? She hadn't finally retired until after Ritchie's father was taken by the yuffids. After Fitz had started his long odyssey of foreign service academies. His school breaks were always too short, and his parents had moved so many times in the years between.

How had he not realized they had never once come back here? Well, his parents had without him, but they had never been here during any of his school breaks. Not even during the unscheduled ones when he'd been kicked out of one school and hadn't yet been accepted to another.

That was starting to feel like it had to have been deliberate.

The music started up again. The speakers were all around the room, but unseen. It sounded close, like he was standing in the middle of an orchestra pit, and yet they were all invisible.

Then his eyes finally caught the flicker of motion as his mother practiced a series of turns, the ends of the diaphanous scarf tied around her hips spinning with her like the fins of some aquatic creature.

Suddenly she stopped, arms counter-turning as she planted her feet and stared down at the floor.

"That's not it," she grumbled mostly to herself, then looked up at the wall of mirrors before her, seeing herself and all the open doors behind her, but not Fitz, who was just out of her line of sight. Then she threw back over her shoulder, "go back twelve bars and hit it again. I'm just going to listen for the rhythm this time."

"Of course, ma'am," her assistant said. What was her name? Viola? Something like that. Fitz took another step into the room and finally found the woman in the far corner, tapping at a wall screen. There was a clicking sound like a drummer counting off beats with their sticks. Then the music played again. His mother stayed where she was, hands on her hips and eyes on the floor, but her head bobbed off a count, and he knew she was imagining the dance in her head.

"Maybe," she said, rising up on her toes, but then settling to the ground again. Her scarf bobbed up then drifted back down with the motion, as did her arms. "Viola, I—" But then she broke off, finally seeing Fitz standing there. "Fitz? Is something wrong?"

"Guardian Wahli let me come down to see you," Fitz said, gesturing back over his shoulder to where the guardian in question was watching from the hallway.

"Ma'am," he said with a nod. "If you can verify all exits are secured, I can leave the two of you alone for a moment."

"Well, I can't exactly do that here," his mother said, indicating all the open doors behind her with a tip of her head. "But we can go into my green room."

"That will work for me, ma'am," Wahli said. Apparently, he already knew that Fitz's mother's green room was an interior room, no windows and only the single door.

"Come along, then, Fitz," she said, reaching a hand out to him.

"I'm not interrupting?" Fitz asked.

"Don't be silly. You know this is just a hobby for me now," she said. As if he hadn't just seen that she took it all as seriously as ever.

"You're sure?"

"Come on," she said, crossing the room to take him by the hand and tow him behind her across the slightly tacky floor to the door on the far side. The room beyond was filled with racks of dancing costumes, and a vanity sat under a well-lit mirror, its surface cluttered with cosmetics and hair accessories, but there was also a small sitting area tucked into one corner.

His mother let go of his hand once they were inside the room and took a seat on the sofa. The scarf flared up again as she turned to sit, then settled around her like the petals of a flower.

Fitz knew he was smiling, but he couldn't help it. Her dance movements were so ingrained she did them without thinking. Every motion was always an exercise in grace and spoke volumes.

But then Viola brushed past Fitz as she came in behind them. She leaned against the vanity, not joining them in the sitting area, but she was still there.

And Fitz was fairly certain she shouldn't be.

He was just about to remark on the Klemm-like hovering, when his mother, as if reading his thoughts on his face, rushed to say, "what can I help you with, Fitz?" Then she patted the seat of the sofa next to her. Fitz sat down, but not beside her. Instead, he perched on a footstool a little further away. It wasn't comfortable at all, but it meant that when his mother was looking at him, Viola couldn't see her face.

Of course, Fitz's would be on full display. But Fitz had no intention of hiding anything. But he was starting to think that his mother might.

"Father isn't here," he said.

"No, he was called away. Military emergency. You know that means he had to leave the governor's residence to tend to it," she said.

"I remember the protocols," Fitz said, although that memory was a dim one. But it was starting to come back to him now.

"He's in orbit, on a military cruiser," she said. "He'll be back as soon as he can."

"Haven't we heard *that* before," Fitz said.

"I expect him back before dinner," she said. "Does that answer suit you better?"

"I like it better," Fitz admitted.

She smiled at him, then smoothed her skirt. But she knew that wasn't what he had come down to ask her. She was still looking at him expectantly. But also nervously.

"Mom, what's going on here?" he asked her. "I mean, this new—"

But she cut him off again, even faster than before, raising a hand to demand silence. Then she turned to look at Viola behind her. "It's nearly lunchtime. All of our guests are still here, and I'm taking longer than expected here."

"I told you your schedule was too tight for dancing," Viola said, her tone gently teasing. But Fitz didn't like it.

"Yes, you were right. But could you please just see how the kitchen staff is doing? I asked them to attempt Nisi souffles, and now I'm worried."

"It *is* a very tricky dish," Viola said with a conceding nod.

"Yes, but it's so important that everyone is comfortable here while they're being detained. Can you just give them a little guidance? You know Nisi culture as well as I do," she said.

Viola looked torn. Like she wanted to insist on staying, but she also wanted to point out that she, in fact, knew more about Nisi culture than her employer did.

"Thank you, Viola," his mother went on, as if Viola had already agreed. "I just need to run through the music a few more times before I take a shower. You are a lifesaver."

"I don't think you're going to get that fourth spin in there, but I'll cover for you downstairs," Viola said, pushing off from the vanity.

"Maybe you're right," his mother said. "Can you start up the music again on your way out? But turn it up so we can hear it in here. Thanks so much!"

Viola just nodded and swept out of the room. The music started playing at once, much louder than before. Wahli was out of sight of the green room doorway, but Fitz knew he was likely standing well out of earshot. So far, his impressions of Wahli were that he was a man of his word.

But clearly his mother was being extra-cautious. Only when he turned to look at her again, she still looked panicked. Like Viola might come back, without warning. Since when was his mother afraid of her own assistant? Viola had been working in the house since she had started interning at age sixteen. She was closer to his mother than he was, in a lot of ways.

"What's going on, Mom?" Fitz asked. "You have to tell me, because I'm really starting to freak out here."

"You can't worry about us," she said even as she scootched closer to him, grasping his hands in hers.

Her hands were shaking.

"How can I not?"

"No, I know. I just mean, you should focus on Ritchie," she said. "Now that you've told her everything, you need to watch out for her."

"I was doing that anyway," Fitz said. "Not that she needs it. Or she didn't until we came here."

"That's going to sort itself out, don't worry," she said. But the shaking of her hands made not worrying an impossibility for him. "You know your father will always look out for her, no matter where she is or where he is."

"I know that?" Fitz scoffed. "Actually, I pretty much know the opposite of that to be true."

"No, I promise you, he's done everything he could to keep her safe," she said.

"Come on. You don't believe that's true," Fitz said.

"We've fought over it, actually," she told him. "There have been times where I felt he was protecting her at the expense of you."

"Seriously?" Fitz asked.

"I can't tell you all the details now. We don't have that much time," she said. "You know your father loves you…"

Actually, Fitz had doubted that very thing on more than one occasion. But this wasn't the moment to say so, especially not to his mother, who hadn't even paused for a breath.

"… but he owes a great debt to Diplomat Ritchie. A debt of honor. And you know what that means to him," she said gravely.

"I suppose I ought to, but honestly, I don't," Fitz said. Which was the plain truth, but he regretted saying it when he saw the hurt in her eyes.

"Oh, Fitz."

"Why can't you tell me what's going on here? Who is this Klemm guy, really?"

"Don't!" she said, with all the firmness he remembered from his early childhood days. "You can't interfere in this, Fitz. You cannot. Just, protect Ritchie. And yourself. That's job enough for you now."

"But something is going on, right?" he insisted.

"Fitz, swear to me. Swear to me now that you won't interfere." She grasped his hands almost painfully tightly as she gazed into his eyes.

She wasn't going to let him go until she had his answer.

"I swear to protect Ritchie and myself first, above all things," he said.

"And not to interfere," she pressed.

Fitz opened his mouth. He intended to argue, but he never got a word out. It was only later that he wondered if his mother assumed he had been about to make that promise that she wanted to hear from him. She certainly released his hands as if she had his vow, smiling up at Viola before that interfering woman was even all the way inside the room.

Fitz felt a little stab of guilt about that. But it wasn't like he could clear up the misconception, not with Viola there.

Not that he didn't intend to keep the promise he *had* made. He fully meant to. He would protect Ritchie and himself, first above all things.

Because if anything happened to either of them, who was going to be left to interfere with whatever dark cloud had settled over his family's home?

21

DURING THE LONG, slow hours of the afternoon, Ritchie realized she had forgotten another aspect of life on a warm planet: the siesta. On Oymyakon, sunlight was too precious to waste on napping. But on Buennagel, the sun was only occasionally lost behind clouds, and even when it was, the humidity in the prairie air kept things warm and comfortable. Almost too comfortable. That warmth plus the monotonous drone of the insects made dozing off almost impossible to avoid.

She might've enjoyed a warm afternoon's nap, if only she weren't desperate to get out of that room and solve a murder.

"Can you all hear me?" said a voice. She sat up and looked around the room, but neither Moreau stretched out on her own bed nor Rodin sitting by the door had spoken.

She reached for her tablet, pretending to scan through a textbook. Technically, she *was* supposed to be keeping up with her assignments even while away from school. That might've fallen to the very bottom of her to-do list, but it made for good cover when Rodin gave her a sharp look, wondering why she had sat up so quickly.

"It's Wyss. On your implants. I know I sound funny. If you ever text-to-speech the messages in your inbox, it sounds like this," he said.

Ritchie realized it was true. She usually put her messages on her visual display so she could scan the text that appeared to be floating in front of her, but on occasion she had set them to fake an auditory stimulus. She had hated that strange voice in her head sensation. But this time, it was possibly the best thing she had ever heard.

"I've taken remote control over your implants for now, so we're all on the same chat channel. I'll have to show you later how to control it yourselves. For now, pretend you're mentally dictating a message. It will go to the channel rather than your outbox. Try it."

"This is weird," Ritchie mentally dictated.

She wasn't sure if she had actually done anything, but she saw Moreau looking at her from across the room, and she knew it was her speaking through the voice in Ritchie's head that said, "tell me about it."

"Are you kidding? If this is secure, this is a game changer for us," the voice said. Ritchie decided that had to be Fitz.

"Can we make the voices sound different?" the voice asked. Sokolov, maybe? Moreau didn't look like she had asked anything.

"Wyss here. I can do that in the future, but it's going to take a lot more tweaking. For now, we'll just have to keep identifying ourselves."

"Fitz here. Are we sure this is secure?"

"Wyss here. It's as secure as I can make it. Which makes it more secure than any existing system known to the Union of Free Worlds."

"He said humbly," the voice said. No identification, but that sounded like something Fitz would say.

"Ritchie here. This is great, but what's our next step?"

"Fitz here. I tried to see my father again, but he and Klemm are up in orbit on a military matter. I don't know when they'll be back, but my mother expected him by dinner. If we mice wanted to play while the cats were away, we have a very short window."

"So we know Klemm is a cat? Oh, sorry, Moreau here."

"Fitz again. I don't know for sure, but there is definitely something going on in my family. Klemm being an evil, interfering influence seems like the most likely scenario. But I don't know how or why."

"Ritchie here. Is Sokolov on the line? I'm curious if she found anything in his office?"

"Sokolov here. There was nothing in his office, but I did find an older model computer in his room, tucked behind a bookcase."

"Behind a bookcase? Nice." No identification, but again, Ritchie was sure this was Fitz.

"Sokolov here again. Yeah, it seemed suspicious to me. Wyss helped me get past the password protection. The files on it were all current, like they had details new since yesterday. And they were all about us. Every single one of our school records, medical history, everything."

"Ritchie here. Why would he have that? Was there any indication?"

"Sokolov here. There was nothing on there but our records, so I don't know what he had them for. But they looked like the sort of background information someone might pull while assessing a job candidate."

"Wyss here. That level of background pull suggests someone is being vetted for a security clearance. Sokolov sent me everything, and I went over it myself. It doesn't feel like someone digging for blackmail or any other nefarious thing I can think of."

"Ritchie here. Are you saying you think Klemm is our contact?" Even thinking that thought out as a mental dictation turned her stomach. "He's being unappealing as some sort of cover?"

"Sokolov here. Stars, I really hope not. I don't think I can get past my bone-deep intuition not to trust him to ever be able to work with him. It just doesn't feel like he's acting."

"Ritchie here again. Any evidence that he might be our killer?"

"Wyss here. Definitely no on that one."

"What could you find in his rooms that would prove a negative? Sorry, Ritchie here."

"Wyss here again. It wasn't in his rooms. I have multiple confirmations of his location for the entire night. He was in the high security room in the sub-basement, with General Fitz and several other officers. He was in that secured space with multiple witnesses from well before until well after the murder. I can't imagine a more rock-solid alibi than that."

"Fitz here. Any idea what they were doing in the room?"

"Wyss here. No clue. I know military matters have to be taken care of off-planet, and planetary matters technically shouldn't involve

Klemm. But that's a minor issue of protocol, and really doesn't affect the solidness of the alibi."

"I was really hoping he was guilty." Ritchie had no idea who said that, but she shared the same opinion.

"Wyss here again. I tracked down Klemm's movements over the entire night of the murder first, but I hit our other suspects as well."

He kept talking, but Ritchie lost the thread of the words when the door to the room opened. The guardian who had been on duty the night before came back into the room, and Rodin got up and stretched the kinks out of her back.

"Shift change," she dictated. The chat fell silent at once. Moreau sat up on her bed, and the two of them watched as Rodin and the new guardian whispered together for a moment. Then Rodin left, taking the lunch dishes with her.

"Ritchie here. Guardian Rodin is gone. We have the guardian from last night here again."

"Wyss here. We good to keep talking?"

"Ritchie here. We're good. Go ahead." She left the tablet on her lap, but she no longer had to remember to tap at it now and again so that it looked like she was studying something engrossing. She could just let it rest there and look like she was daydreaming. The guardian made a pass around the room, bathroom and balcony, then went back to turn the chair towards the door once more.

"Wyss here. As I was saying, Henri Schor never left the Schors' room at all that night. That's absolutely confirmed. But Abilene muted all of her implant functions."

"Fitz here. What does that mean?"

"Wyss again. It means she was even more invisible than Ritchie usually is. I have no idea where she was physically. For six hours, she was basically a ghost. Invisible to security. She could've gone anywhere. Unless her husband was awake and saw her leave or return, and will testify to that fact, I'm not sure what that gives us, besides more suspicion."

"Fitz here. We saw that murder scene. Do we really think that woman was capable of that?"

No one spoke.

Finally, Ritchie dictated, "we don't need more suspicions. We need more proof."

"Fitz here. Suspicion isn't useless. But we do have too much of it. Ritchie, the guardian in your room felt like an ally last night." Ritchie felt her cheeks heat, the way he just casually mentioned that to everybody, as if he didn't need to explain how they knew that. But he kept going. "Something is going on in this house. She might be a good place to start figuring out what that is. I mean, I tried just asking my mother, but that was a non-starter."

Before Ritchie could respond, Moreau leaned forward, elbows on the knees of her crossed legs, chin in her hands. She gave the guardian at the door her brightest smile. "You were here last night, but I never asked your name?"

"It's Guardian Thalmann," she said, turning away from the door to look at the two of them. "Cadets Moreau and Ritchie. I know you."

"Yeah, I guess we're kind of famous," Moreau said.

Thalmann laughed. "Maybe not in a good way, cadet."

"Oh, sure. This is just a temporary misunderstanding though, right? I mean, you know we didn't do anything to hurt anyone."

"Rules are rules, cadet. Especially when you wear a uniform," Thalmann said almost harshly.

"Rules are rules, but right is right and wrong is wrong. And sometimes the rules are secondary to that," Moreau said.

Thalmann considered this, but just shrugged.

"Fitz is worried about his parents," Ritchie said.

Thalmann looked over at her, and Ritchie could see the sorrow there lurking in her eyes.

"He's right to be. Isn't he?" Ritchie guessed.

"As a guardian serving this governor, I can't speak to that," Thalmann said. Very carefully, Ritchie noted.

"Can anyone?" Moreau asked.

"No, I don't think anyone can," Thalmann said. Then she sighed and rubbed at her own cheeks. Her eyes were red-rimmed, and her skin had a pale, tired look to it.

"Are you doing all right, Guardian Thalmann?" Moreau asked.

"To be honest, I think this is one too many extra shifts for me," she said, and slouched back low in the obviously uncomfortable chair. "It's a good thing your parole is secure. I would hate to think what could happen if I dozed off, and you were free to move around the building. That could be bad."

"Um, Moreau to Ritchie, I guess. Is she inviting you to escape? Because I think she's inviting you to escape?"

Ritchie had to agree. She just wasn't positive it wasn't some kind of trap.

"Fitz here. What's going on?"

"Ritchie here. Guardian Thalmann here just heavily implied that if my parole wasn't working, I could slip away and she wouldn't do anything about it."

"Wyss here. For what it's worth, your parole *isn't* working. I disabled it just now."

"Fitz here. Ritchie, I know you hate the idea of someone messing with your implant without your knowledge, but you know Wyss only wanted to help."

"Yeah, Fitz, I know that," Ritchie thought/dictated. "But now what?"

"Moreau here. I think now Ritchie and I slip out while we can."

"Sokolov here. What will you do once you're out? We already searched the cottage, Klemm's rooms and the Schors' room. What else is there?"

"Ritchie here. The bedroom in the cottage. We never actually went inside it."

"Fitz here. The window is still open."

"Wyss here. Fitz is correct. I can also get you past the security measures. It will appear on the logs if anyone checks later, but no one will be notified right away. If you find something, hopefully how you found it won't matter."

"Moreau here. Hopefully, we find something."

"Ritchie here. Moreau and I are on our way to the cottage."

"Fitz here. How are you intending to do that? The corridors and elevators are all being watched by security. Even with your parole removed from your implant, you'll be seen."

Ritchie couldn't help grinning, as odd as it must've looked to be smiling fondly down at her homework. "Ritchie here. Fitz, you have climbing gear in your rooms, right? From our bouldering days? Moreau and I just need enough rope to get down from one balcony to the next."

Instant response: "Fitz here. I don't like this idea."

"Moreau here. Tough. We've got this. And we're in a hurry." Then she got up from her bed and gave Ritchie a conspiratorial wink.

"Guardian Thalmann? Permission to take some air out on the balcony?" Ritchie asked as she too got up from her bed and stretched out her back.

"Permission granted, cadets. Take all the time you need," she said. Then added, almost as if she were speaking to the room at large, "I sure do wish I had some coffee. It's going to be a long night without it."

They stepped out onto the balcony at the same moment as Fitz did on his side of the dividing wall. He was carrying the rope, but he was clearly not happy about handing it over.

"My guardian is definitely not an ally," he grumbled, looking back over his shoulder. "He brings in backup when he needs to take a bathroom break. Luckily, this rope was in the same chest as this old thing." He held up a boomerang, scuffed after years of being jammed into that overly full chest. But when Fitz threw it off the balcony, it arced perfectly and circled back to be caught by him again. "At least I have an excuse to be out here for a bit. I can watch you go, even if I can't join you."

He threw the boomerang again with one hand, giving Ritchie the bundle of rope with the other. She took the rope, waited for him to catch the boomerang, then pulled him down to give him a quick kiss before he could throw it again.

"Thank you, Fitz."

"Just be safe," he grumbled.

"Safe and hopefully a little lucky," Ritchie said. Then she and Moreau started taking turns lowering each other balcony by balcony, all the way down fourteen levels to the grasslands below.

22

FITZ STAYED out on the balcony long past the point where Ritchie and Moreau had passed out of sight around the corner of the building, towards the path through the hills that led to the cottage. The sun sank ever lower in the sky behind him, but still he kept throwing that boomerang and catching it, throwing and catching it.

The guardian mumbled something to himself about cabin fever, but Fitz found him easy enough to ignore.

But then, as the last rays of the sun were winking out of sight, the door to his rooms burst open and he heard a voice he was never able to ignore. His father.

And the voice of his father was dismissing the guardian.

Fitz caught the boomerang one last time, then came into the room again to find the guardian just on his way out, closing the door behind him. He hadn't even put up a fight. Maybe he *had* been an ally after all.

"Father?" Fitz said, dropping the old boomerang back into the storage chest and kicking the lid closed. Then he noticed something else, something he really should have noticed first. "Where's Klemm?"

"Never mind that now. There isn't enough time to explain every-thing," his father said. He grabbed Fitz by the arm and dragged him back out to the balcony. He was looking everywhere with an almost manic level of paranoia in his eyes.

"It's okay. Wyss swept my rooms for bugs yesterday. Shortly before you had us all put under house arrest," Fitz said. He hoped not too bitterly.

"Have you been here every minute since that sweep?" his father asked him.

"Sure," Fitz said. Then he remembered. "Well, except for that one time, I went to talk to Mom."

His father thought this over, then nodded. "Wyss is good. We'll trust that."

"Well, like you said, I wasn't here the whole time," Fitz said.

"Then we'll just have to pray no one was here while you were not," his father said.

Why did that make his blood run cold? The idea that his father would admit there was something outside of his control? Something they'd just have to hope went their way? His father? The one who verified everything but preferred if he could control it himself?

"What's going on here?" Fitz asked. After asking so many times, he had no expectation he would get an answer this time either.

But then his father said the very last thing he ever thought he'd hear. "I'm your contact."

"My contact?" Fitz repeated.

"All of you," his father said. "That's why I brought you all here."

"I thought you brought me home because I violated my parole while being investigated as a possible murder suspect?" Fitz said.

"You certainly gave me the perfect cover for meeting with you. I couldn't pass up the opportunity to make good on that," his father said. He sounded odd. Almost... proud?

"Wait," Fitz said.

"Sorry, son. I know this is a lot to take in, but we really don't have a lot of time. I truly am your contact, here to meet with all five of you. I had hoped to have more opportunity than it turned out we've had. In my defense, I had hoped to send Klemm away on a separate mission, but the murder of Diplomat Lavatar made that impossible."

"Wait, what?" Fitz said. "This is crazy. What's this about Klemm?"

"It's not safe to discuss him here," his father said, lowering his voice to a whisper and looking around with that paranoid glow to his eyes again.

Only Fitz didn't think he was being paranoid. Fitz was starting to realize his father's over-zealous need for security precautions was maybe not paranoid enough.

"Klemm knows," Fitz said with complete surety. His father gave him a questioning look, but Fitz just held up a hand, gesturing for him to stay silent.

Then he started dictating a message to the chat channel. "Fitz here. Wyss, can you add my father to this?"

"Wyss here. Are you sure that's wise?"

"Fitz here. I trust him. But I really need to talk to him. Securely."

"Wyss here. Hold on. I'll set up a separate channel for the two of you."

"Three of us. I want my mother in on it, too."

"Wyss here. Your father should be on with you in a second. I'm muting you on the other channel so you don't get an overlap. Moreau and Ritchie have reached the cottage, and Sokolov and I are assisting their search."

"Fitz here. Sounds good. Let me know…"

But he didn't need to finish his thought. He saw the very instant his father could hear the voice inside his head by the way his eyes suddenly lit up. Wyss hopped on to explain everything to him, and Fitz just waited for him to finish. He looked out over the twilit meadows and wondered how Ritchie and Moreau were doing.

What could they possibly hope to find that the investigators didn't? And yet they had nowhere else to search for clues.

"General Fitz here. Cadet Wyss, are you absolutely certain this channel is secure?"

"Wyss here. A few of the things I built on are known to others working on the bleeding edge of the tech, but I think I've progressed further than even they would think possible. No one knows what I'm doing is even achievable, or how to detect it happening if they did, let alone know how to breach it. Sir, I can think of no safer way to communicate."

"General Fitz here. That's good enough for me. More than that, it's outstanding work. This is a real game-changer for our side."

"Wyss here. Thank you, sir. I'm bringing your wife into the chat now."

"Hello?"

"Luana, it's Shackleton. Fitz is here as well."

There was a lot of cross-talk that Fitz couldn't follow before Wyss got his parents calmed down again, clear on the rules of waiting to speak and identifying yourself before speaking. Then he had to explain all over again how he knew their communication was secure.

And Fitz just waited. Impatiently. He was tempted to ask Wyss to unmute him from the other conversation so he could hear how Ritchie was doing, but that would mean interrupting and making all this take longer. All he could do was wait.

"Wyss here one last time. I'm monitoring two channels, so be sure to holler loud if you need my attention."

"General Fitz here. Understood, cadet. Fitz, are you still on?"

"It's in my head, Dad. I can't turn it off."

His father, standing before him, looked startled. Then he blinked hard, as if holding back tears.

Then Fitz realized what had happened. He hadn't called his father "Dad" in years. It had just slipped out. But his father had definitely noticed.

"Luana here. That's how this works? Are we really sure this is safe?"

"Fitz here. There's some risk. Is anyone around who might notice you're acting oddly?"

"No, I'm alone. For now."

"Shackleton here. Fitz is right. We have to be sure when we use this, it looks like we're doing something else. Lu, you usually communicate through a tablet as well as your implant. That will be your cover if you need it."

He didn't have to add that he, as a general, not only was adept at using his implant without drawing notice, but that he did it constantly. Even while in conversation with others.

Still, Fitz worried that Klemm might somehow still be able to tell. Because Klemm always watched so very closely.

"Fitz here. So Klemm is definitely a spy, then?"

"Shackleton here. Yes. No question. Not the first to be embedded in our household, but definitely the best."

"Mom here. He has recruited a number of the staff here as well as at our other homes. We know it's a lot of them, but we don't know how many or who we can still trust."

"Shackleton here. We do know the latter. Trust no one save each other."

"Fitz here. How long has this been going on? Since you said Klemm wasn't the first."

His father gave him a look of great sorrow. "Fitz, you know how long. You know exactly how long."

"Mom here. Your father worked very hard to protect you from all this. Getting you into early programs in the foreign service academy wasn't exactly easy. If you had picked a military career, you could've saved us both so much stress and worry. We would have had so much more control."

"Lu, the boy has to chart his own path."

Fitz rubbed at his forehead, completely disoriented. Everything he had thought was true about his parents was exactly backwards?

"You sent me away for my own good?"

"Shackleton here. Son, if you weren't here, no one would try to use you as a conduit to intelligence about either of us. But especially me. It hasn't been easy, keeping you at arm's length. But it has been necessary."

"And Ritchie?"

There was a long silence, broken at last by his mother saying, "tell him, Shackleton."

"It is going to take hours to explain it all. But, Fitz, I've changed my mind about her."

"She's not all bad, right?" Fitz said, a bit annoyed that the voice that read his dictation conveyed absolutely no sarcasm whatsoever.

"Fitz, I thought she would be safest far, far away from this world we live in. But in the last few years, I've seen that keeping her safe can't be my primary objective."

Fitz realized the lack of tone in the voice in his head was also stripping his father's words of important subtext. Because as cold as those words sounded in his head, the look on his father's face was something close to grief.

"I don't understand," Fitz dictated.

"I can't keep her safe because we need her. Her skills, her abilities. We can't do this without her."

"Who's we?"

"Those of us who still believe in the original mission of the Union of Free Worlds. Those who believe that all should be welcome, as difficult as that can be among species so very divergent. Those of us who believe that war is only a means of last resort, never the first answer to conflict."

"Fitz, he means all of us who have allied against the Admirals Berweger and their kind." That had to be his mother speaking. Fitz rubbed at his head again. This implant talking was giving him a headache. But he had so many more questions.

The breeze that was dancing through the waves of grass suddenly built up into a gust that blew coldly across Fitz's back. It tickled something like a chill up his spine. But that chill triggered a thought, the sort of thought that really should've triggered that spinal chill, like a reverse stimulus-response. But that thought was a long time coming.

He should've asked it first thing when it was safe to speak, but he had forgotten it.

"Dad, where's Klemm right now?"

His father frowned thoughtfully. "He said he had a personal matter to deal with."

"Isn't that odd?"

"I really don't know, Fitz. He just said he had a few loose ends to tie up. I didn't ask what he meant."

Fitz rushed to the railing and looked out over the grasslands. The sun was long gone, but the moons had not yet risen. There was absolutely no way he could see anything, let alone see the cottage beyond the hills.

But he really wished he could.

"Fitz?"

Fitz turned back to look at his father, then spoke out loud. "Ritchie is in danger."

"How…?" his father started to ask, but before he could finish, they both heard the voice in their heads once more.

"Wyss here. Fitz, Ritchie is in trouble."

Fitz gripped the railing with numb fingers. He should've asked at once. He could've been down there by now. How could he have forgotten about Klemm, even for a minute?

But his father grasped his arm and started tugging him towards the door.

"Come on. We can take the elevator straight down to ground level, but we'll have to run from there."

Fitz wanted to feel the happiness of being on the same side as his father, something he never thought he'd feel. But his fear for Ritchie was too overwhelming.

He ran.

23

RITCHIE AND MOREAU slipped into the cottage through the kitchen door and were confronted at once with the smell of dried blood. It was still thick in the air, coppery and sticky. Ritchie supposed that was a good sign. If the crime scene hadn't been cleaned up yet, there still might be something up there to find.

Not that she held onto a lot of hope. She knew the guardian investigators would have been very thorough. Best-case scenario would be if they found something the guardians had also found but hadn't understood the significance of.

Not that she had any idea what that could be.

"Ready?" Moreau asked.

"As I'll ever be," Ritchie said, then led the way upstairs to the closed bedroom door. Once upon a time, this had been her parents' room. It had been off limits to her without permission as a kid, their private space. Strangely, that lingering respect for her parents' wishes was the hard part to get her head around now. The fact that it was sealed against anyone but those guardians with the appropriate security clearances didn't bother her nearly as much.

"Wyss here. You're both on the security list now. You should be good to open the door," the voice in her head said.

Ritchie looked to Moreau, who gave her a nod of encouragement. Then Ritchie put her hand on the cold metal doorknob and turned.

The door swung open easily, revealing a room all in shadows. Some starlight faintly brightened a patch under the open window, but with neither moon yet up, there was barely any illumination at all.

"Ritchie here. Wyss, can I use night mode on my implant? Or will that trigger something with my parole?"

"Wyss here. You're fine to use night mode. I disabled everything when I shut down your parole. Nothing you're doing now is even showing up on the activity logs. The security guardians are only seeing the fabricated data I'm sending them. You're in your room with Moreau, chilling."

"I'm already in night mode," Moreau said to her. "It's probably better if we don't turn on any lights, just in case someone is out there that might notice."

"That's what I was thinking," Ritchie said. With a sigh, she mentally reached out to her implant and toggled her night vision on. Now the shadows around her brightened, then gained definition. She could see the outline of the bed, currently stripped of bedding. That was probably in an evidence bag back at the guardian headquarters in the subbasement of the governor's residence. Along with the drapes that should be hanging over the window.

But the walls were still splattered with darker gray streaks. Ritchie was grateful that the lack of color in her night vision took some of the edge off of the horror around her. Not that she could even for a second stop smelling it.

"No clothes in the closet," Moreau said as she poked around the far corner of the room. Ritchie dropped to her knees to look under the bed, but there wasn't so much as a dust bunny under there. She opened the drawer in the night table, but it was empty.

Ritchie sat back on her heels and looked around the room. Then she dictated, "Ritchie here. Wyss, is there any difference here from when your drone was recording?"

"Wyss here. Actually, there is one change. There was a chair in the corner between the bed and the window that's gone now. It was quite blood-soaked, more even than the mattress is now."

"That's something," Moreau said, getting up on tiptoes to try to peek to the back of the shelves at the top of the closet. "At least we know they're still working the case if they came back for more evidence."

"If that evidence had told them anything or even just opened another line of questioning, Wyss would already know about it, though," Ritchie said with another frustrated sigh. "This isn't panning out. There's nothing here."

"Don't give u—" Moreau started to say, then broke off in a high shriek of terror.

"What?" Ritchie demanded, lunging to her feet and bolting to the open doorway. But there was nothing there. She turned back to see Moreau standing on the blood-stained mattress, eyes huge as she tried to look everywhere at once. "What is it?" Ritchie asked again.

"Something touched me," she said in a harsh whisper.

"What touched you?"

"Something in the back of the closet," Moreau said, pointing. "I thought it might be a clue, this little dark shape in the deepest corner of the closet. But when I touched it, it touched me back."

Ritchie crossed the room to look into the closet herself. There was nothing there. She dropped into a low squat again, running her hands along the baseboard next to the floor, but she felt nothing.

"Is it gone?" Moreau asked.

"It seems so," Ritchie said, and Moreau stepped back down off the bed with a thump. Ritchie couldn't imagine what could be so terrifying that standing on that murder bed would seem the better option. "You grabbed it with your hand, so it was small?"

"Small and dark," Moreau said. "It was warm and furry, but when I grabbed it, it squeaked at me and bit me." She held out her hand. Ritchie had to peer closely to see the little pinpricks at the base of Moreau's thumb.

"It broke the skin, if only a little," Ritchie said.

"Why are you so calm?" Moreau demanded.

"Moreau, it was probably just a field mouse," Ritchie said. "Obviously, it's more scared of you than you are of it. It thought you were going to squeeze the life out of it. Of course, it had to bite you to get away."

"Field mouse," Moreau said, as if the words meant nothing to her.

"Sure. It's a little early in the season for them to be moving indoors. They usually do it when the nights start getting longer and colder. But every fall when I was a kid, we'd have to set traps and keep an eye out, especially in the kitchen." Ritchie crept inside the closet to take a better look around.

"Every year you dealt with this?" Moreau asked with a shudder.

"Well, I never tried picking one up," Ritchie said with a grin. "Where did this one go?"

"I don't know. I dropped it and got out of there as fast as I could," Moreau said.

Ritchie put her hands on the smooth floorboards and dropped her head down until she was eye-level with the baseboard. Then she saw it, a tiny crack in the deepest corner where two baseboards met but didn't quite join. Ritchie crept closer to it, poking a finger inside.

"Watch it!" Moreau warned her.

"It's fine. It didn't run back in here," Ritchie said. "But it did leave something behind. A nest of sorts." She took a multi-tool out of her cargo pocket and used it to pry one of the baseboards away. Then she could see the little nook in the wall that had been lurking behind it. "Yep. Definitely a nest."

"Please tell me it isn't full of babies," Moreau said.

"No babies. There is something in here, though," Ritchie said. Moreau made a low moan of protest as Ritchie put her face even closer to the hole in the wall.

"What is it?" Moreau asked when Ritchie was still for far too long.

"I don't know for sure, but I think it's hair," Ritchie said. She poked at it a bit with the end of her multi-tool, but didn't dare touch it. Enough of her DNA had ended up in the wrong places already.

"Mouse hair or human hair?" Moreau asked. Her curiosity was getting the better of her, chasing the last of her repulsion and fear away from her voice.

"Human," Ritchie said. "Try to stand between me and the window, will you? I need a little proper light to get a good look at this mass. Night vision isn't telling me enough."

"Okay. I'm ready," Moreau said, arms wide as she tried to make herself unfurl like a privacy screen.

Ritchie found the light function on her multi-tool and clicked it on.

The hair in the hole in the wall was a fading shade of blonde, brittle-looking and more yellowish than gray.

"Well, this is a conundrum," Ritchie said, switching off her light again and shifting her weight to sit back on her heels.

"What's that?" Moreau asked.

"It's Abilene Schor's hair, I'm sure of it," Ritchie said. "I'm just not sure how that mouse got a hold of it."

"If she was here, maybe she just shed it?" Moreau suggested. "It wouldn't be the weirdest thing in the world for the wife of a diplomat to call on another diplomat socially."

"Sure, but it's a lot of hair," Ritchie said. "An entire lock of it, roots and all. And there's a little bit of blood on the roots, like they were pulled out forcefully."

"By who?" Moreau wondered.

"That's the conundrum," Ritchie said, looking up at her. "Did she actually kill Diplomat Lavatar? In which case Heidi Lavatar might have pulled out that chunk of hair while she was fighting for her life?"

"Or was it planted, like your DNA on that knife?" Moreau asked.

"Exactly," Ritchie said.

"But she does have those unaccounted for hours on the night of the murder," Moreau went on. "I know she doesn't look like she could do… all this," she said, waving her hands at the blood-spattered walls around them. "But that doesn't mean she didn't."

"Or, like me, someone is trying to frame her," Ritchie said. "She seemed like a tedious woman, but she was drinking at the time. And the investigators have questioned her at least once and opted not to detain her. I don't know."

"So what do we do?" Moreau asked. "How can we tell if she's guilty or not?"

"We can't. Not from this," Ritchie admitted. "But either way, we have to let the guardian investigators know they missed this. There's nothing we can do with it ourselves, anyway."

"Let's update the others," Moreau said.

Ritchie nodded, then stood up before dictating. "Ritchie here. We found some of Abilene Schor's hair. It looks like it was pulled out of her head by the roots. Either she was here or someone is framing her. I don't think there's any way for us to tell which is which."

"Wyss here. There's another problem with Abilene Schor as the killer. The security systems that were hacked to let her in. There is nothing in any of her records to indicate she has that level of skill. And her academic career was so mediocre, and so long ago, I have a hard time imagining her acquiring that skill on her own."

"Moreau here. Doesn't mean she couldn't, or didn't."

"Wyss here. Agreed. But it's not the likeliest scenario."

"Ritchie here. So she's not our suspect?"

"Wyss here. I'm not saying that. It certainly looks like she was at least there, in that cottage. But if she did it, she didn't act alone."

"Great, another conspiracy," Ritchie grumbled. But Moreau was staring at the door to the hall, and she was shifting her body into a defensive posture. Ritchie turned to follow her gaze and saw Klemm standing in the doorway, staring at the both of them.

That creepy feeling she hated, the one she felt every time he was watching her, struck with double force, as if making up for that second or two she hadn't felt his eyes on her.

But she forced herself to set that aside for a moment. What if her instincts that he was not to be trusted were wrong? What if he was watching them all the time because he really was their contact?

She could only suspend that instinct for an instant. In the end, she agreed with Sokolov. No one was such a good actor that they could trigger that instinctive distrust at will. Although if they could, it would certainly put them above suspicion for being a collaborator with the non-evil side of this conflict.

Klemm said nothing to either of them, just watching them with that inscrutable look on his face, like he was waiting for them to speak first.

"Lieutenant Klemm," Ritchie said. She had to swallow hard before she could go on. "I suppose you're wondering what the two of us are doing here."

"No," he said. "I can see what you're doing. You're violating your parole. And you were warned of the consequences."

"I know, but..." Ritchie began. She didn't know what she was going to say next, how she was going to save her future career from this black mark. She didn't have Fitz's family's power to fix things for her, but she had to say something in her own defense.

She realized too late, however, that Klemm wasn't talking about any sort of black mark on her permanent record. He was talking about what he, as a security officer, could do to someone who was violating an implant parole.

She didn't remember anyone warning her about it. She had a split second to remember something Fitz had said about the pain when he had tried to walk into a crime scene while his own parole was active.

Then there was nothing but pain, blinding pain coming from within her own head. She screamed and fell to her knees. She could feel Moreau's hands trying to catch her, to pull her back up, but it was like it was happening to some other body. All her own body could feel was that pain radiating through her, over and over again.

She lost all sense of time as she desperately wished she could just pass out, to lose all awareness of everything but, most of all, of the pain.

Somewhere distantly she heard voices. Familiar voices. Then, like someone had thrown a switch, that pain was gone.

And instantly she got her wish. Before she could even open her eyes or hear who it was that was around her now, her consciousness slipped away into a warm and welcoming oblivion.

24

FITZ WAS WINDED by the time the cottage came into view. It looked unoccupied, no light in any of the windows, no sound but the drone of the nighttime insects in the grasses around them. It seemed safe to slow down to a walk now that they were nearly there. And as tired as he was, his father beside him was more so.

Then he heard a scream. Ritchie's scream. And suddenly he was sprinting again, vaulting over the raised beds of the kitchen garden and into the dark cottage.

He charged up the stairs to the still-unlit bedroom where he knew she had to be. His father was in the cottage now too, but had slowed his steps at the bottom of the stairs. Fitz heard him subvocalizing as he gave someone orders over his comm, but he didn't pause to find out more. He took the steps two at a time and burst into the bedroom to find Ritchie curled up and shrieking on the floor. Moreau was trying to calm her, but Ritchie twisted away from her hands, contorting in pain.

And standing over them both was Klemm.

Fitz didn't even think about it. He just spun Klemm around, then clocked him straight in the face. Klemm's knees buckled, and he dropped to the ground.

But Ritchie never ceased screaming.

"Make it stop," Fitz demanded. Klemm snuffled on the blood that was flowing from his nose and glared up at Fitz, but said nothing.

"He's doing something to her implant," Moreau said, still trying helplessly to hold Ritchie still. "But Wyss disabled her parole. What's he doing?"

"Answer the question, Klemm," Fitz said, grabbing Klemm by the hair and raising his fist threateningly. Not that he really wanted to hit Klemm again. His hand was already throbbing from the first blow. But he had no weapon on him.

"Answer the question, Lieutenant Klemm," his father said as he suddenly appeared in the doorway.

"She is violating her parole by being here. I merely reactivated the protocols," Klemm said, and spat a glob of blood onto the floor.

"Security is on their way here now. She will be back in custody soon enough," Fitz's father said. "You can stop this now."

Klemm said nothing, but the corner of his lip curled up ever so slightly in the faintest hint of a sneer.

The room suddenly filled with light as a hopper dropped onto the meadow just outside. Boots ran up to the house, then in through both front and back doors. Two heartbeats later, four guardians with stun pistols raised burst into the room. One of them was Rodin, but another was Wahli.

"They're here now, Klemm. Release Cadet Ritchie," Fitz's father said warningly.

Klemm said nothing.

"Sir?" Guardian Wahli asked, unsure what to do.

"We take the cadet into custody, correct, sir?" Guardian Rodin said. She dropped to one knee, trying to grab Ritchie by the arm to pull her to her feet. But Ritchie's body was rigidly curled in on itself, and Rodin couldn't even get a grip on her.

And Ritchie never stopped shrieking. Even as they could all hear how it was shredding her vocal cords.

"Dad, please," Fitz said.

"Guardians, arrest the lieutenant," Fitz's father ordered. "Take him into custody, now."

Rodin openly gaped at the general, the disbelief on her face so prominent it had to be real. But there was fear there too. Whatever she knew or suspected about Klemm, she knew he was not to be trifled with.

The two guardians nearer the door shifted their weight from foot to foot and moved their stun pistols around without committing on who to point them at.

But Wahli bent to take Klemm by the arm. One of the guardians by the door made a decision and rushed to help. Soon, Klemm was out of the room, then out of the cottage. They loaded him into the hopper and jumped away, back towards the governor's residence, even as a second hopper landed with more guardians to supplement the remainder of the first team.

And still Ritchie was screaming.

"We have to do something," Moreau said, unmindful of the tears running down her own face as she tried once more to get Ritchie to focus on her.

"Wyss!" Fitz bellowed.

"I'm working on it. I'm trying to figure out what Klemm did. Some sort of back door—"

"You have to do something, now!" Fitz cried. "You have no idea what she's going through."

"Actually, I can see it better than you can. I'm in her head."

"Then do something!"

"I'm working on it. The only way to do it faster is to shut down her whole implant."

"Then do that."

"I don't know what that will do for her long-term, Fitz. It might be really bad."

"Wyss, *this* is really bad," Fitz said. He realized he was snuffling too, but unlike Klemm, it wasn't blood he was choking on. "Just do it."

The scream cut off abruptly, like someone had shut off an audio playback. Then all the tension went out of Ritchie's body and she was a limp puddle on the floor.

"Ritchie. Ritchie?" Moreau called, shaking her buddy's shoulder.

Fitz dropped to the ground beside the two of them, but he didn't dare touch Ritchie. Like it would make it all too real, whatever was happening.

He felt completely useless.

"Sir, we found this woman hiding in the other bedroom," a guardian in the hallway said to his father. Fitz turned around to see two guardians with Abilene Schor between them. Someone had turned on every light in the place, and Fitz hadn't even noticed.

Abilene looked inside the room, but not at Ritchie. She was grimacing at the blood splatter on all the walls as well as the ceiling. She looked shocked and repulsed. But those emotions didn't extend to her eyes. No, he saw fear in her eyes. And it wasn't his father who she was afraid of.

"Mrs. Schor. Would you care to explain what you are doing in this cottage?" his father asked coldly.

"No, I don't think I would," she replied, lifting her chin defiantly.

But that fear was still there. And it was making her voice waver ever so slightly.

"Lieutenant Klemm is in custody. You're safe now," Fitz said to her.

His father shot him a questioning look. But then he turned his attention back to Mrs. Schor. She was visibly shaking. "Were you being held here against your will? I beg you to be honest with me."

"I have nothing to say to you," she said, thrusting her chin up a little higher. Fitz wanted to press her for more, but his father just sighed and turned away from her.

"Take her back to the holding cells," his father said with a dismissive wave. "Where are the two I sent to fetch a stretcher?"

"Just here, sir," someone said from beyond Fitz's field of view.

"Lovely. Get this woman in the hopper in full restraints," his father commanded, and the two in the hallway dragged Abilene Schor out of sight. Then the other two came in with the stretcher. Fitz got to his feet, gently pulling Moreau out of the way so the two guardians could move Ritchie's inert form onto the stretcher.

"She's barely breathing," Moreau said.

"We have medical equipment on the hopper, and we'll be back at the residence in minutes," Fitz assured her. But he knew he sounded more optimistic than he felt.

"Abilene Schor is either the killer, or she's being framed like Ritchie," Moreau said, wiping her nose on her sleeve, then instantly pulling herself back together.

"You're sure?" his father asked even as he turned to give her his full attention.

"Pretty much. Ritchie and I found a tuft of her hair in a field mouse nest at the back of the closet. It was pulled out by the roots. Someone authorized for evidence collection should retrieve it, actually. And check the logs to see if it was missed before or planted since. Neither of us touched it," Moreau said.

Fitz's father turned to give Guardian Rodin a nod, and she pulled a bag out of her pocket and headed towards the closet.

"Are we sure we trust her?" Fitz asked, then immediately regretted not asking over the secured chat channel.

"Guardian Rodin? Certainly," his father said. Fitz raised an eyebrow, but his father just nodded again. Fitz shrugged. Not every person who rubbed him the wrong way was working for the enemy, he guessed. Some of them were just annoying.

"Let's get to the hopper so we can get Murdina to the infirmary as soon as possible," his father said, and neither Fitz nor Moreau had to be asked twice. They followed his father out to the hopper and climbed aboard. It was tight quarters inside, especially with two guardians ministering to Ritchie, whose stretcher took up most of the space.

Then there was Abilene Schor, who looked very small indeed tucked away in the back corner. She was shackled hand and foot, and those shackles were attached to a retaining bar set into the bench she was sitting on. She wasn't going anywhere. But she didn't look like she was planning an escape. She looked like she was about to burst into tears.

"All here," Fitz's father said to the driver as he closed the door behind all of them. The hopper rose up on its jointed legs, then started back towards the residence. Despite its name, it was a smooth ride, the legs propelling it along in perfectly horizontal jumps.

"You will soon be charged with the murder of Heidi Lavatar," his father said to Abilene. She blinked at him in feigned surprise.

"I'm sure I have no idea how your people came to that conclusion, general," she said. They could all see her hands were shaking, and she carefully folded them together to hold them still.

"But even if you did it, you didn't do it alone," his father went on. "There is no reason for you to be charged with more than you actually did. If you even did anything at all. I have my doubts. If you're just honest with me, this will go much better for you."

Abilene Schor swallowed several times, as if she didn't trust herself to speak. When at last she got up the nerve, lifting her chin once more, her voice was mostly warble-free. "I swear I'm being honest with you, general. There is no one else to be charged but me."

"What do you mean?" Fitz demanded.

"I did it all. All on my own. I killed Heidi Lavatar. There, that's my confession," she said. She was gaining confidence now.

"How?" Fitz asked.

"What do you mean, how? Haven't you already worked all that out?" she asked.

"How did you get in and out of the cottage without triggering the security notifications? How did you ambush Diplomat Lavatar? How did you cut her over and over without killing her too quickly?" Fitz demanded.

Moreau gasped and put a hand on his arm, silently begging him to stop. His father was scowling at him. But Abilene Schor looked like she wanted to vomit.

Which would be bad. There wasn't anywhere in that tight space for that to go except over everyone else huddled together in there.

"No more questions," Fitz's father said. "Mrs. Schor, you will be taken to an interrogation room when we arrive at my residence, and you will be questioned there very, very thoroughly. I do hope you will answer my investigators more honestly than you have answered me and my son."

"I'm being completely honest, general. I did it. And I did it alone. And that's all I have to say on the matter," she said primly. She seemed to have found some hidden reserve of strength within herself, a place of cold formality and misplaced moral superiority. She wasn't going to change her story. But he knew in his bones her story was a lie.

The hopper came to a halt on the gravelled ground in front of the main doors, and Fitz's father opened the door, jumping to the ground then turning to help the others. Fitz and Moreau stood out of the way, watching as Abilene Schor, head held high, was led into the main hall and then down into the subbasement.

Then Ritchie on the stretcher was eased down to the ground. Moreau and Fitz fell into step behind it, following the guardians who carried her to the infirmary. It took Fitz a moment to realize his father was there with them.

"Don't you have to go question that Schor woman?" Fitz asked him.

"The investigators have it for now," Fitz's father said.

"And Klemm?" Fitz pressed.

"I want to see Murdina settled first," his father said.

"Dad, I'll watch out for Ritchie, okay? I need you to stay on Klemm," Fitz said.

His father gave him a funny look, and Fitz realized he had kinda, sorta just given his father, the general, an order.

Then they reached the infirmary to see Wyss and Sokolov already there, waiting for them.

"You're right, son. Especially about Klemm. There is a limit to how long we can hold him, and that clock is ticking even as we speak. But I'll be back as soon as I can," he promised.

He left, and almost as if that had been a cue, the medics immediately sent the rest of them to a waiting area while they worked on Ritchie. The cadets could watch on a screen as attempts were made to rouse Ritchie, but they weren't allowed to even try to help.

It was more than an hour before the medics gave up. They kept Ritchie attached to every piece of monitoring equipment they had, then summoned the cadets back into the room.

"We've done all we can," the woman in charge said to them. "The general suggested there might be something a Cadet Wyss can try?" She didn't sound optimistic.

"Maybe," Wyss said. "I don't know if I should, though."

"Well, I'll leave you all alone with her for a few moments and you can discuss it," the woman said. "Call if you need me sooner."

Wyss just nodded, distracted. Fitz murmured a thank you to the medic as she left the room, closing the door behind her.

Moreau was sitting on the side of the bed, holding tightly to Ritchie's hand. Fitz stayed where he was, leaning against the wall beside the door with his arms crossed tightly.

He didn't know what else to do.

"Maybe she'll wake up on her own?" Sokolov suggested. She was examining the readouts on the machines as if they meant something to her. Maybe they did. But nothing Fitz had learned in field medic class had covered anything like this.

"Wyss, what is it you aren't sure about trying?" Moreau asked.

"I shut down her implant, the entire thing," Wyss said. "There's a procedure for that if it's medically necessary. Sometimes things go wrong and they need to replace an implant, right? Only I didn't follow those procedures. I just pulled the plug. Metaphorically speaking."

"So you can plug it back in?" Fitz asked, not daring to hope.

"I can try restoring the power and rebooting the systems," Wyss said, but too slowly.

"But?" Fitz prompted.

"But the damage might be permanent. She could be stuck like this forever," he said miserably.

Moreau brushed the hair back from Ritchie's pale face, then adjusted the blankets around her as if to make her more comfortable. As if Ritchie could notice or care.

Fitz wished he could do that. But he couldn't seem to move from where he was.

"The damage from what might be permanent?" Sokolov asked. Wyss gave her a questioning look. "The damage from turning the implant back on? Or from shutting it down? It just seems to me, the damage is already done. Trying anything now, could you really make it worse?"

"Things can always get worse," Fitz said.

"No, Sokolov is right," Wyss said. "Turning it back on has risks, but nothing like what I already did to her. I should just try it, right?"

"Try it," Moreau said firmly. Then she reached a hand out towards Fitz. She wasn't looking his way. It was like she didn't dare take her eyes off of Ritchie's face for even a moment. But something about that outstretched hand unstuck Fitz from the wall. He crossed the room to

Ritchie's bedside, and Moreau got up and gently pushed him down in her place.

"Okay, I'm rebooting it now," Wyss said. As far as anyone else could tell, he was still just standing there. He didn't even have a tablet in his hands. He was doing it all from his own implant, invisibly.

Or he was doing nothing at all. After several more seconds ticked by, that started to feel like what was going on.

Then the limp hand Fitz held in both his own suddenly grasped at him tightly. Ritchie sucked in a long breath, like she had just come up from a deep dive underwater.

And her eyes fluttered open.

"Murdina," Fitz said, forcing a smile on his face, although terror still gripped his heart. It was those two words haunting him still. Permanent damage.

Was she okay?

"It's Ritchie to you," she said. Her words were a little slurred, but her eyes were bright. Moreau squealed in delight and starting hugging/dancing with Sokolov. The two of them pulled an unwilling Wyss into their clinch. Only Fitz was close enough to hear Ritchie add, "you wanted it that way."

"You are correct. My apologies," Fitz said, but brushed a few stray strands of hair away from her eyes, anyway. "My partner, Cadet Ritchie. Soon to be Guardian Ritchie."

"You know it," she said. Then there was a mischievous gleam in her eyes. "Unless you want me to start calling you Shackleton?"

"Ugh. *No.*"

"It's a nice name," she said. "It has a rich history, you know."

"I know. Just… it's Fitz. Always has been," he said.

"Always will be," she finished for him.

25

RITCHIE WASN'T EVEN able to get out of bed yet before they were on their way back to Oymyakon. She didn't know exactly what had happened between the time when Klemm had used her implant to cripple her with pain worse than anything she had ever even imagined was possible and when she had woken up to Fitz's anxious face so close to hers.

She at least understood that Klemm was in custody, and they were safely out from under his watchful gaze. But that wouldn't last for long. Something about the only thing he could be charged with was overzealously enforcing a parole, and how his lawyers were really the Berwegers' lawyers and hence some of the best in the Union of Free Worlds.

Fitz's family's lawyers were almost as good. They had negotiated dropping the charges against Klemm in return for dropping the charges against Ritchie for violating her parole, and apparently also for Fitz punching Klemm in the face.

Ritchie was sorry she had missed that.

In the end, Klemm was going to go free. He wouldn't even be removed from the Fitz household. He would just go on spying and whatever else he was doing while embedded there. And there was nothing even General Fitz could do about that.

But negotiations took time, even if it was only a few hours. Fitz's father made the most of that time, having his guardians take Ritchie back out to his shuttle on a stretcher and hurrying the other cadets to follow behind. If they were gone from Buennagel before Klemm was released, they would still have the flight to Oymyakon to talk freely.

Ritchie drifted in and out of involuntary naps, never quite catching what conversations were going on around her. She would occasionally focus on a worried face and try to force herself into a bit more wakefulness. But she never managed more than a few minutes.

Then suddenly she was just awake. The cabin around her was dark, although she could hear the others were still there, sleeping on the folded-down chairs. She heard Moreau's gentle snoring for sure.

She freed herself from the monitoring equipment, then swung her bare feet to the soft carpeting of the shuttle floor. She made her way to the bathroom easily enough, then found her own bag so she could change into a clean uniform rather than the infirmary gown she was still wearing.

But the first thing she saw when she unzipped her bag was her old tablet, the one she had found in her childhood bedroom. Someone, she suspected Fitz's mother, had made sure it was packed with the rest of her things to go back to school.

And under the tablet was a little tin filled with Maiden's Breath, the candy she used to make with her mother after they had distilled all the Immerweis blossoms. This candy looked factory-produced, all uniform and individually wrapped, but it was still a very welcome gift. It would be the perfect antidote to a typical Oymyakon cold, wet afternoon. She couldn't wait to share it with all her friends.

She was just debating finding something to eat a little more substantial than candy when she noticed a light at the end of the corridor that ran down the center of the shuttle from fore to aft. It was further back than the berths that were reserved for family use. But it had become suddenly bright because a door that had been closed when she sneaked into the bathroom was open now.

It was like it was calling to her. She headed towards it.

"Ah, Cadet Ritchie. Feeling better? Excellent," Fitz's father said, glancing up from his desk when she appeared in his doorway.

"Yes, thanks," Ritchie said, touching her forehead as if what had happened to her might have left some sort of visible mark. But of course it hadn't. "Fitz told me how his implant had kept him from crime scenes and other places back on Braga when he was under parole, but I think he undersold it a little."

"No, he did not," Fitz's father said. "What Klemm did to you was beyond what implants are even supposed to be capable of. Wyss is going to have to stay on his toes if he's going to keep our systems secure against Klemm. The two of them are both scary smart. It's going to be a very different sort of arms race."

"Hopefully, the difference is that Wyss has friends he can call on for help," Ritchie said. The general raised his eyebrows, and she quickly waved her hands. "Not Fitz and me! I mean other friends. Super-smart people who trade knowledge with him. I don't know them personally, but I know he doesn't do anything entirely alone."

"I think you are correct. That is a significant difference between them," he said. "But I must apologize for putting you in danger. I knew Klemm was likely the reason so much evidence was pointing to you as the killer of Diplomat Lavatar. And I knew he was a danger, just in a general sense. But I let my guard lapse, and you were hurt. I'm sorry."

"I don't think you could've really known what would happen," Ritchie said.

"I should've known," he sighed. "I don't know if the others told you yet, but I am your contact on Braga next year."

"Oh," Ritchie said, surprised. "No, they hadn't mentioned that."

"Yes. Everything that happened to you on Buennagel is really my fault. I had hoped to send Lieutenant Klemm away so that I could speak with you all without fear of being caught, but he was suspicious the minute I suggested he take on the mission I was using as a pretext. I know that now; at the time it was not remotely clear."

"Why is that important?" Ritchie asked.

"I think he had Diplomat Lavatar killed simply so that he would be compelled to stay here despite my orders," he said.

"That's horrible," Ritchie said. "It's just so random."

"Well, not entirely," the general said. "He never wanted her in that position. He saw an opportunity to achieve two objectives at once."

"But we know he didn't do it," Ritchie said. "Wyss said he was with you the entire night. A rock-solid alibi."

"Yes, he was with me. He didn't do the wet work himself," he said. Then he just looked at her, waiting for her to put it together.

But she already had. "Wet work," Ritchie said. "The part of spycraft that deals with assassinations and, I guess, murder in general. Right?"

"Right. We'll never know how much he did himself. Was he just the planner, or did he take down the security systems himself? We may never know."

"But the guardian investigators will find out, right? They will work the case," Ritchie said.

"Not when they have a confession," he said.

"Abilene Schor confessed? Why would she do that?"

"I don't know. But she radiates fear. I don't know what Klemm threatened her with. Her husband's life, possibly. But she won't waver. And as improbable a suspect as she is for what happened in that room, she can speak to every detail. It makes no sense, but that won't matter. Not when the Berwegers have lawyers on both sides of the question steering the entire course of the inquiry."

"The hair was planted later?" Ritchie said.

"We can't prove it, but my gut says yes." Then he shifted his weight in his chair, dangerously close to fidgeting like Fitz would do. "I also have to apologize for not realizing sooner what Klemm was up to when we returned from orbit. He told me he had a personal emergency that needed his immediate attention, and I was thinking too much about how this finally gave me a minute alone with my son to realize the personal emergency was you."

"That's why he was at the cottage," Ritchie guessed.

"I'll never know for sure, but I fear he was there to kill you and frame Abilene Schor for everything," Fitz's father said. "It had become clear to him that framing you was never going to work. Not in my house, anyway. So he switched tactics. All I know for a fact was that he received a notification the moment that Cadet Wyss removed your parole. Everything else is guesswork on my part. But I'm sure enough that I'm right that I know I owe you an apology for my misjudgment."

"Well, again, I don't know how you could've known what would happen," Ritchie said.

"Still," he said. Then he gestured to the chair set opposite him at his desk. "Won't you sit? I know you're feeling better, but you should still not be pushing harder than you have to."

Ritchie had to admit she did feel a little lightheaded. "Thanks," she said, and slid into the seat.

"Tea?" he offered, half-turning towards the replicator in the corner of his office.

"And sandwiches?" she asked hopefully.

"Of course," he said, and pushed a few buttons. Ritchie soon found herself staring down a mountain of sandwiches, more than twice what she could possibly eat. She looked them over, choosing one that was oozing melted cheese to start with.

She felt like she hadn't eaten in days.

"I have more to apologize for, of course," he said as he settled back into his seat.

Ritchie froze halfway through biting into the sandwich. She had wanted to have this conversation for so long, but now that it seemed to be starting, she had the sudden urge to run away. But she held her ground, swallowing down the bite of sandwich before saying, "please don't tell me that you were trying to protect me. Because that doesn't make anything better."

"No, I can see how it wouldn't," he said. "I tried to keep you away from things, and I'm sure to you that felt very controlling."

"You kept me out of the foreign service academies even though I was more than qualified," Ritchie said.

"I did," he admitted.

"To keep me away from Fitz?"

"No. Well, that was part of it," he conceded. "I just wanted to keep you safe. I thought that was the best way. You had figured out something you shouldn't have, and that put you in danger. But I wasn't paying attention to how mature you were. I could've trusted you, maybe all along I could've trusted you. But I wasn't close enough to you to see it."

"I was right," Ritchie said, and made the gesture that would've calmed the yuffids, three fingers under the chin, if her father had only done it.

"You were right."

She appreciated that he wasn't trying to defend himself, but a little more explanation wouldn't exactly be a bad thing. "Why didn't you tell him, then? You didn't think I was right at the time? Because I was just twelve?" She could hear her voice choking up and set the mostly uneaten sandwich back on the plate with the others.

"No, on the contrary. I knew when Fitz told me that you were right," he said.

"So you deliberately didn't warn my father?" she demanded.

"I didn't have to. He already knew," he said.

"What?" Ritchie stammered. "Why? If he already knew how to avoid offending them, why didn't he do it?"

"It had to be convincing. When they took him. And it was. The Berwegers have figured out so much that we thought was secret, but that they haven't the slightest suspicion about. No, every spy we've put on them has said the same thing. They gloat about it. They treat it as some great joke that just proves how right they are about human/alien relations. But never once have they considered that it was staged."

"I don't understand," Ritchie said.

"The Berwegers want open war with an alien species. They want to use that as a pretext to remove every other non-human species from the Union of Free Worlds. And the yuffids, being so easily offended and nearly as quick to declare wars as humans are, were the perfect species for their plans."

"Okay, but how does what my father did help? At all?" Ritchie demanded.

"Because he's not dead. He's a prisoner," Fitz's father told her. "As long as he's alive, and the reason he was taken wasn't in battle but in the midst of a cultural misunderstanding, by the Union of the Free

World's own laws, that's a diplomatic matter, not a military one. And it has a diplomatic solution."

"He's not dead?" Ritchie asked. She swallowed hard. "You know that for a fact?"

"I do," he said, his eyes suddenly kind. "Nothing broke my heart more than that moment when Fitz came to me and told me what you had figured out. Because not only did it mean that you would know something was wrong when your father was taken, but if you ever said a word about it, the Berwegers would know, too."

"You sent me away to keep my quiet?" she asked.

"I sent you away so that if you did say anything, the Berwegers wouldn't hear. Or so I hoped. They have spies everywhere. I didn't know for sure that you would be safe. But you would be safer than you would be on Buennagel."

"There were spies here, even then?"

"Even then," he agreed. "Even knowing exactly what he is, I can't remove Klemm. I need the Berwegers to think they know everything I know. So Luana and I live pretend lives, and we keep you and Fitz as far away as we can."

"Fitz never knew? That it was all staged, I mean," Ritchie said.

"He never knew. He knows he told me what you told him, and that I did nothing with that information. And after your father was taken, I told him not to say a word about it to anyone, especially not to you. I had to let him hate me for that. And other things."

"And my father is for sure still alive?" Ritchie said. She could say it out loud over and over again, but it never seemed to feel real to her. Not yet.

"He is alive," Fitz's father said. "And from time to time I can get messages to him, and vice versa."

"But you can't bring him home?" she guessed.

"Possibly I could, but it's not time for that yet. He's not ready."

"What do you mean?"

"Your father was taken for a reason, remember?"

"To stop a war, I thought," Ritchie said. But that didn't make sense. He had done what he did the way he had to prevent a war that other methods might provoke, but that wasn't *why* he had done it. "What's the real reason?"

"His job," Fitz's father said. "Negotiations with the yuffids have continued, just in a different guise. He is a prisoner from the UFW point of view, but from the yuffid point of view, he's something more like… an involuntary guest."

"How is that different?" she asked.

He laughed and shrugged. "Your dad can explain the nuance better than I. The long and the short of it is that he can still speak as a diplomat to their own diplomatic leaders. He is still negotiating for the yuffids to join the Union. Until he either succeeds or decides it's all hopeless, he will stay there as their guest. Or hostage, as the Berwegers believe he is."

"That's crazy," Ritchie said, touching her forehead again. "But I guess I can see why it's true."

"I know I don't understand all the nuances. It's a kind of diplomacy I have no experience in. Their culture is so very alien to us."

"Well, that's what we have diplomats for," Ritchie said. "Was Heidi Lavatar meant to help?"

"She was," Fitz's father said, and a sadness touched his eyes. "She will be very hard to replace. Which is exactly why Klemm had her eliminated."

"Sidonie Keller was obsessed with the yuffids," Ritchie said. "Still is, from where she's being held and observed. A shame she's too crazy to be let out. Ever."

"Yes. But there are others," he said. "They need more training, but there are candidates."

A long silence stretched between them before Ritchie broke down and said, "I thought you were going to pressure me to go to diplomat school just now."

"I think you would make an excellent diplomat. In fact, I'm certain you would become exactly the sort of diplomat I'm looking for," he said.

"But what? You can't wait that long?" she guessed.

"Partly. Mainly, your decision to go to guardian school is so unexpected. I know the Berwegers are baffled by it. They don't know how to counter it." Then he gave her another sad look. "I'm afraid Finn Berweger is going to be even more of a problem for you in the future, when you are both on Braga."

"I can handle Finn," she said. But she wasn't sure if that were true. And she really didn't look forward to testing it. He had managed to blow up her relationship with Guy Travert with scarcely any effort at all.

And she really didn't want to think what Finn would do if he knew how she felt about Fitz. Kissing Fitz had solidified feelings she only thought she had before. And Finn would know something changed the minute he saw her. He would guess. And he'd use that, somehow. Use it against her, or use it against Fitz.

Fitz, who only wanted them to work together as partners. She was still adjusting to that idea, too.

At least she had something else to focus on now. Something huge.

Her father, still alive.

"Well, as baffled as the Berwegers are with the idea of you becoming a guardian, I find it very interesting indeed. I'm familiar with your skill set and qualifications, but I can't wait to see how you apply all of that to guardian school."

"I'll do all I can," Ritchie said. "I'll figure out a way to help my father."

"Oh, I have no doubt you will," he said.

26

FITZ WOKE to the sounds of his father laughing.

Laughing? His father? That never happened.

Even more puzzling, the person laughing with him was Ritchie.

Fitz sat up, throwing the blanket he had curled up under aside, and leaned out into the corridor. The door to his father's office was wide open, and the light spilled out onto the far wall. He could definitely hear Ritchie and his father talking and laughing together. He caught enough words to realize they were talking about him. The time he had fallen into a vat of chocolate as a child.

That hadn't been funny! The chocolate had still been hot, and he had burned his arms and legs. Not seriously, but it had still hurt quite a bit. And no one had let him lick any of it off his skin.

Then Ritchie stepped out into the corridor and Fitz sat back in his chair, feigning sleep as she walked by, passing him to head straight for the replicator. He was sure she was dialing up breakfast, and knowing her it was going to be a mountain of scrambled eggs cooked in butter.

As good as that sounded, and as much as he wanted to talk to Ritchie, he still had unfinished business with his father. He looked back over his shoulder, but Ritchie was preoccupied with the replicator. Fitz hoisted himself out of the depths of his seat and launched down the corridor to the office door.

"There you are," his father said without looking up. As if he had expected Fitz to turn up at precisely this moment, in the small hours of the morning.

"Ritchie seems in good spirits," Fitz said, as he sat down across from his father. He knew he sounded suspicious. But that's because he *was* suspicious.

"Well, why wouldn't she be?" his father asked. "I was just showing her Cadet Wyss's project list."

"Sure," Fitz said. He was familiar with it. Wyss was driven to give them all, but especially Ritchie, complete control of their own implants. They would be unhackable for real this time. Not even the government could touch them. More than that, they would all be much more active users. Wyss was convinced that passive use created just the sort of unthinking dependence that made the implants so very dangerous.

Not that he was likely to explain it to Ritchie that way.

"I'm not sure what Wyss had to say about that chocolate vat, though," Fitz said.

"Yes, right," his father said with a chuckle. "It's possible the two of us got a little off topic at the end there."

"So she's just cool with you?" Fitz demanded. "All is forgiven?"

"Maybe not all," his father said. "But she understands now."

"Well, I don't," Fitz grumped.

"Don't you?" his father said. "I thought I explained. The meet that Ritchie's father had with the yuffids was set up by the Berwegers. They wanted to see him fail, fail spectacularly."

"And that's not what they saw?" Fitz asked.

"They wanted to see him dead," his father told him. "That's not what they got."

"They sure seem to think they won something that day," Fitz said.

"Because Ritchie's father and I staged things to make them think so," his father told him. "In fact, her father is still there, among the yuffids, negotiating for the Union."

"And the Berwegers don't know that," Fitz guessed.

"If they did, they would put a stop to it," his father said.

"And then Ritchie's dad really woud be dead," Fitz said.

"We're working to make sure that doesn't happen. Among other things," his father said.

"I don't think you needed to do everything you did to make that happen, though," Fitz said.

"You think I was too hard on you?" his father asked, raising a single eyebrow.

"I was talking about Ritchie," Fitz said.

"I've discussed this with Ritchie," his father said with a dismissive wave. "Now I'm talking to you, about you."

"Okay," Fitz said, not entirely sure he knew what that meant.

"I *have* been harder on you than I needed to be," his father said, to Fitz's complete surprise.

"You're admitting that?" he asked when he finally got his hanging jaw back under his control.

"I was harder on you in each moment than that particular set of concurrent circumstances made necessary," his father said.

"Whatever that means," Fitz grumbled.

"It means I *had* to be harder on you, because I knew better than you what your future held for you," his father said.

"That's kind of condescending," Fitz said. "I always knew I was going to inherit the governorship of an entire world. As ridiculously outdated as that concept is."

"That's not what I meant," his father said. "I meant Ritchie. Your friend. I knew better than you what she was going to face. And I knew even when you were twelve that whatever she was meant to face, you'd be facing it right there with her. Tell me I'm wrong."

"You certainly tried hard enough to make that not happen," Fitz pointed out.

"Not everything worked out like I wanted. I'll admit that," his father said. "And I already admitted to you that I underestimated Murdina Ritchie."

"But?" Fitz said, sure there was more that his father was avoiding saying out loud.

"I know she'll step up for the challenges ahead," his father said. "I wish I could say I was as sure of you."

"Thanks, Dad," Fitz said. Ritchie was a star in his father's eyes now, and that was at it should be. His father had nothing but praise for Wyss, and that too was only appropriate. Even Sokolov had impressed him when he'd seen how her close working relationship with Colonel Hansen had led to her nearly being able to read the colonel's mind.

But Fitz? Fitz was still worthless in his own father's eyes.

Unless this was another one of those "harder than he had to be" moments?

"Well, like you said, I'll always do whatever it takes to be at Ritchie's side through everything. So that hasn't changed," Fitz said.

"I suppose we'll both just have to trust that is enough," his father said.

"It's been almost two years since I've been expelled from a school, you know," Fitz felt compelled to point out.

"Ritchie's influence. We shall just have to wait and see if it carries you through four years of guardian school. Because there's nowhere else for you to go if you get expelled from there."

"I know that, Dad," Fitz said.

His father nodded, then picked up a tablet and began very pointedly reading. Fitz huffed out of the office to find Ritchie standing in the corridor with two bowls of steaming scrambled eggs in her hands.

"I knew you weren't really sleeping," she said as she handed one to him.

"Can't get anything past you," he said as he took it, then followed her to a little table set apart from the rest of the cabin where the others were still sleeping. She dug in at once, but he just poked at his. Finally he asked, "so, we're okay?"

"I think so," she said.

"We're not just setting it aside for later? Because we found the killer, kinda, and now we're going back to school," he said.

"We're okay," she assured him. "Although now that you mention school, I have some suggestions for changes to your schedule."

"What are you talking about? It's our last semester. Coast!" he said.

"Not with the independent study curriculum I'm setting up for us to pursue at guardian school," she said between bites of egg.

"Independent study? Isn't that a diplomat thing?" he asked, wrinkling his nose in distaste at the very concept.

"I'm bringing a little diplomat energy to the guardian school," she said with a shrug. "And we have a lot of work to do. You and I, if we're going to figure out a way to rescue my father. Not just extract him from the yuffids, but help him achieve his objective first."

"How are we going to do that?" Fitz asked.

"First, we study," she said, and set a tablet in front of him. "Which starts with getting rid of your coasting schedule. You need some higher level classes now, so you'll be at my level next year at guardian school."

Fitz looked at the tablet but didn't touch it.

"Unless you changed your mind?" she asked. Then she started to pull the tablet back towards her end of the table. "I guess if I'm in this alone—"

"Come on. You know you're not," he said, slamming his hand down on the tablet and wrestling it out of her grip. "Give a guy a second to adjust, will you?"

"Sure," Ritchie said, taking another bite of her eggs. But she could scarcely chew, grinning like she was. "I can spare a few seconds. Maybe."

"I'll catch up," he insisted. Then he scanned the list of classes. He was adding more than he was dropping. But she surely knew that already. He sighed. "I'm going to need some help."

"Of course," she said. "That's how this works. Being partners."

"Right. This guardian school has no idea what's coming for it when we get there," he said.

"Ritchie and Fitz. We investigate murders," she said.

"And fight conspiracies," he added.

"But we keep that part on the down low?" she suggested.

He sighed dramatically. "Okay, for now. But soon, everyone is going to know."

"When my dad is free," she said.

"When your dad is free."

27

FITZ'S FATHER landed the shuttle near the train platform, out of sight of the Oymyakon Foreign Service Academy. Ritchie was pretty sure this was Fitz's doing. Landing near the hangar—or, worse yet, the athletic fields—drew far too much attention from the rest of the cadets. When they descended the ramp, they found Colonel Hansen standing alone on the platform, waiting to greet them. The skies were dark and ominous, and the wind was wickedly sharp, but neither rain, snow, nor anything in between was falling.

Yet. Ritchie doubted Hansen was wearing his waterproof squall gear for fun.

"Welcome back, cadets," Hansen said as they gathered around him to drop their bags and dig out their coats. They had gotten off the shuttle subconsciously expecting Buennagel weather, or perhaps the warmth of Braga.

"Colonel Hasen, correct?" Fitz's father said as he came down the ramp behind them.

"That's correct. General Fitz?" Hansen said, thrusting out a gloved hand for the general to shake. "It's nice to finally meet you."

"Likewise," Fitz's father said. "I need to be off at once, cadets, but I will be in touch whenever it is safe for me to do so. In the meantime, I leave you in the best of hands."

"Thank you, sir," Ritchie said, and the others murmured their own gratitude. Fitz hesitated, then gave his father a very brief hug that seemed to catch the older man off guard. But it was done before anyone could react, and then the ramp was drawing up again behind the general's heels. They all stepped back to the far side of the platform as the shuttle engines revved back to life and it lifted off into the air.

"I can see why he was in such a hurry," Wyss said. "I don't like the look of those skies."

Ritchie followed the direction of his gaze and saw a dark bank of roiling clouds building to the east. "We should get inside," she said.

"What time even is it?" Fitz asked as they jogged as quickly as they could up the side of the mountain.

"Just after lunch. You're really too late to join the first afternoon class, so we'll have a debrief in my classroom before you head out to your second afternoon class," Hansen said.

Then they all fell silent as the first fat drops of rain pattered loudly down on their hoods.

Ritchie hesitated, then gathered up her courage and accessed her implant. She still hated using it, even though Wyss had spent the entire trip from Buennagel strengthening all of her security measures. It was safe enough to trust for ordinary use in checking her schedules and messages and the like. He was still working on the deeper functions that required more intimate contact with the networked systems, like research requests or live mapping. But he would have them secure before she needed to use them, she was sure.

She had messages. A lot of messages. Most of them were from the school, and she felt a little guilty for how little she had tried to keep up with her assignments. The next few days were going to be hard, and the semester was only going to build from there.

Not that she could complain. Not after she had just thrust Fitz into the academic deep end. Of course, helping him was going to add to her workload as well. But she couldn't complain. She had to set a cheery example.

She scanned through the rest of her messages. One from her mother, another from her grandmother. Nothing alarming there.

But she had four messages from Finn Berweger. *That* was definitely alarming.

And she had a single message from Guy Travert.

"Everything all right?" Fitz asked, leaning forward as they walked to peer inside the depths of her hood.

"Fine," she said, dismissing all of her messages for later. She would have to deal with all of that later. Much later. After a lot of thought.

What would she have to do with Finn's messages? That gave her the most anxiety. Was she going to have to maintain a close bond with Finn, like Fitz did with Feena? She hated the idea, but she could see the strategic use of it.

What should she do with the message from Guy? She didn't think she could resurrect that relationship now, even assuming that was what he wanted. She hoped he was just looking to stay in touch as friends. Friends she could handle.

Friends she was going to *need*.

But she couldn't think of either of them now. Not until she sorted through her complicated feelings about Fitz. Fitz, who wanted her always with him. But who didn't want a deeper relationship with her.

He had stepped away from her so far, so fast. The memory of it still made her ache.

Even though she knew he was right. And more, that she had so much else to focus on now than silly teenaged stuff.

They reached the library doors and dried off in the airlock before continuing on through the empty library and down the long main hall to Hansen's classroom deep within the mountain itself. In the quiet out of the wind, Ritchie realized that Wyss and Hansen had been talking the entire time about what Wyss was working on.

"And it's going well?" Hansen asked, looking back at Ritchie.

"So far," she told him. "It feels different in my head. More secure. But maybe that's just me imagining things."

"No, I don't think so," Hansen said. "You are far more aware of your implant than most, thanks to what's happened to you. You're an excellent choice as first subject for Wyss's tests. Both because you provide better feedback to him, and because I know we'll all rest more easily knowing your mind is officially off limits to the Berwegers."

"Yes, sir," Ritchie said, not quite sounding as glum as she felt. With her mind better protected, there was no way she *wasn't* going to be put up against Finn as soon as it was practicable. She would just have to get used to the idea.

Hansen unlocked his classroom, and they all filed inside to their usual places. Ritchie realized that this place felt more like home than the cottage back on Buennagel. Sitting at the desk looking up at Hansen, it just felt like where she belonged.

But she would be leaving it soon. In just a few months.

"Right, I trust you enjoyed your second warm planet visit in a row," Hansen said, looking at Ritchie, then Fitz, then Moreau. "It's time to buckle down and prepare for the next battle."

"I think we're ready," Fitz said. Then flushed a little and amended, "by which I mean we're mentally prepared to get prepared. Mentally."

Hansen said nothing, just raised a single eyebrow.

"I couldn't put it better myself," Moreau said sardonically.

"First off, Sokolov," Hansen said. "You will have noticed I've put large blocks of independent study on your schedule."

"Yes, sir. Office hours, sir?" she asked.

"You'll be working in my office, yes, but the two of us are going to be cramming every subject we can. It's time you caught up with the other cadets in your year," he said.

"I don't even know what year that is," Sokolov admitted. "I take classes with almost all of them."

"I'm looking for you to graduate next year. A year at diplomat school without you is all I want to subject Moreau to," he said.

"Sokolov is going to be a diplomat?" Moreau asked. "She's decided already?"

Ritchie could tell from the tone of her voice that she thought Hansen was pushing Sokolov into it, and Moreau absolutely did not approve.

But Sokolov turned in her desk to look at Moreau. "I knew before I came that's what I wanted to do. I'm not guardian material at all.

Although," she added with a blush, "I didn't think I was far enough along academically to even think about diplomat school."

"You'll be ready. We have a year and a half together to make it so, cadet," Hansen said.

"You'll make it," Ritchie assured her.

"So I'll be graduating with Wyss," Sokolov said brightly. But then her face fell as everyone around her sat in uncomfortable silence.

"Yeah, I don't think I'm going to make it that long," Wyss said. "That's why I've been working at this implant problem so hard."

"They could take you at any time?" Fitz asked. He sounded appalled, and Ritchie realized that he had never had a buddy for as long as he had been buddies with Wyss. If Wyss was taken away before the end of the year, Fitz would be buddyless again.

"Probably not this year," Hansen told them, his voice low and grave. "But early next year at the latest. In my experience, he'll likely be taken while on the inter-semester break."

"Wyss, you'll be all alone," Sokolov said with deep sympathy.

"I'll be okay," he said.

"You'll be fine," Hansen said confidently. "We'll miss you. *I'll* miss you. All of you. This place isn't going to be the same without the five of you."

"There'll be other cadets, sir," Fitz said.

"Yes, but they won't be the same. I knew that from the minute I met four of you on that first railway ride here," Hansen said. "One of you not even a cadet yet. But you are all exceptional."

"You're going to swell Fitz's head, sir," Moreau said, although she too was practically preening from the compliment.

"Yes, we wouldn't want that, would we?" Hansen said with a dry grin. "I just hope I've given you all everything you'll need to tackle your futures."

"You have a few more months to pack the rest in, sir," Fitz said.

"Speaking of packing it in, I see there have been some modifications to your schedule," Hansen said to him. "I hope you haven't bitten off more than you can chew."

"Ritchie is going to help, sir," Fitz said.

"Of course she is," Hansen said.

Their implants notified them that the first afternoon class was over and the next was about to begin.

"You should all head to your classes. Time to start catching up," Hansen said, pushing away from his desk and brushing his hands together as if dusting them off.

"You all go ahead," Ritchie said, when the others got up from their desks. Moreau and Fitz gave her wondering looks, but left without further prodding.

"I thought you might want to have a word," Hansen said, unsurprised that she lingered in the room.

"About my father," she said.

"And how much I knew?" he finished for her. She nodded. "Honestly, until General Fitz messaged me from his shuttle on your trip back, all I knew was the public version of events."

"But you've been working with him for some time, haven't you?" Ritchie asked. "The general, I mean. In the resistance, or whatever we're meant to call it."

"I have," he admitted. "I've known for some time that there were threats lurking within our own government, within our military, and within our foreign services. In a way, I've been working with the general for years now, but only very loosely. We've been working more closely since you and Fitz arrived, out of necessity. But I was never told anything about the circumstances surrounding your father until now."

"How is that possible?" Ritchie asked. "Isn't saving him the entire point of everyone's mission?"

"Alas, not remotely," Hansen said. "I've been dedicated to rooting out corruption in the foreign service academies. And you and Fitz have done more of that than I've managed so far. Others I've worked with have had similarly smaller missions."

"But the war with the yuffids? Aren't we all trying to prevent that?" Ritchie asked.

"We're trying to prevent a needless war with any alien species," Hansen said. "They are only one of a myriad of possible conflicts."

"But surely they're the most likely?" Ritchie pressed.

"That's how it looks now, at least to General Fitz," Hansen said. "I don't dispute his reasoning. It is sound from where he stands. But he's only one perspective. From other perspectives, other threats look primary."

"We could get my father back and still not fix what's wrong in the Union?" Ritchie asked, feeling more depressed than ever.

"Fixing what's wrong with an organization the size of the Union is far beyond what any single individual is able to do," Hansen said. "Rescuing your father is a noble goal, and one well worth your pursuing it. And I mean to help you all I can, now and in the future."

"Well, I know I have you to thank that I even have that future," Ritchie said. "Without your intervention, I'd still be back on that over-crowded space station with my mother and my grandmother, completely unable to help anyone at all."

"Oh, I think you'd have found another way out, but even so I am glad to be of service," he said. Then he looked at her with almost an impish gleam to his eye. "And you're about to learn what being of service truly means."

"Sir?"

"I've seen Fitz's schedule changes. They have your fingerprints all over them," he said.

"Wait until you see what I have planned for next year, sir," she said.

"It's going to be a lot of work, keeping him at your level," he said. "Don't you dare drop down to his."

"Fitz's level isn't below mine, sir," Ritchie said. "Academics are only one measure. Maybe not even the most important. But for what we need to do in the future as guardians, we have to have those academic measures in place to get the right opportunities. And I know Fitz will be pulling me up just as much as I help him."

"Perhaps you're right," Hansen said, but he didn't sound convinced. Then he gave her a little nod, pointing his chin towards the door. "You should get going or you're going to be late, cadet."

"Yes, sir," Ritchie said, and headed out the door into the hallway, where only a few other equally late cadets were hustling in both directions. She checked her schedule but not her implant's map. She could find the classroom on her own here on Oymyakon, and by the time she was in Braga's less familiar surroundings, Wyss would have her implant as secure as it could be made.

And when she got to this classroom, Fitz would be there waiting for her. He needed her there to get through the class. And she needed him for so many other things. The two of them together would be stronger as guardians than either one of them alone could ever be. That had to be enough for her now.

But anyway, she knew they had a whole future together to figure the rest of it out. A future that stretched out ahead of her for as far as she could see. A future with Fitz always by her side.

Ritchie and Fitz will return…

NEW SERIES: THE FORGOTTEN PLANET

Coming soon from Ratatoskr Press Books, the new YA sci-fi series *The Forgotten Planet* starts with book 1: *Raiding the Forgotten Derelict.*

History sleeps beneath them all, but only she sees it.

Lafayette Eloi always knew her parents thought differently from others. They kept their books buried beneath her mother's house. They spoke an old language in the dead of night, whispering behind closed doors and bolted shutters. She grew up in a village where no one was related to her, and she never knew why.

Then, after her mother died, her father came to fetch her. Now she and her mother's dog assist her father in his work. The work discussed in whispers in the dark. The work that had cost Lafayette so much all her young life.

But now she learns just how much her father's work means to their entire world. Only no one knows anything about it. Only her father. And only Lafayette.

Because the work that consumed her father's entire life and her mother's too now nibbles at the fringe's of Lafayette's own life. And she cannot refuse its call.

Raiding the Forgotten Derelict, first book in the new YA sci-fu series *The Forgotten Planet,* available in September 2024 from Ratatoskr Press Books.

COMPLETE SERIES: THE RITCHIE AND FITZ SCI-FI MURDER MYSTERIES

The Ritchie and Fitz Sci-Fi Murder Mysteries starts with *Murder on the Intergalactic Railway*.

For Murdina Ritchie, acceptance at the Oymyakon Foreign Service Academy means one last chance at her dream of becoming a diplomat for the Union of Free Worlds. For Shackleton Fitz IV, it represents his last chance not to fail out of military service entirely.

Strange that fate should throw them together now, among the last group of students admitted after the start of the semester. They had once shared the strongest of friendships. But that all ended a long time ago.

But when an insufferable but politically important woman turns up murdered, the two agree to put their differences aside and work together to solve the case.

Because the murderer might strike again. But more importantly, solving a murder would just have to impress the dour colonel who clearly thinks neither of them belong at his academy.

Murder on the Intergalactic Railway, the first book in *The Ritchie and Fitz Sci-Fi Murder Mysteries*.

COMPLETE SERIES: THE TRAVELS OF SCOUT SHANNON

The complete six-book series *The Travels of Scout Shannon* begin with book one, *Under Falling Skies.*

Scout Shannon's whole family died the day the Space Farers dropped an asteroid on their domed city. Now she lives alone, out in the wild with only her dogs for company. She prefers it that way.

But Scout finds herself at a crossroads. One road leads back to a quiet life snug under the protective dome of a city. The other road leads to a life in the rebellion, a life of adventure and excitement but also danger. Dare she try to find the rebels hiding in the hills?

Then a chance encounter with a stranger from the other side of the galaxy threatens to derail what remains of Scout's life. The entire galaxy awaits her, if she survives the next four days.

Under Falling Skies, a young adult science fiction novel, set on a remote planet with a distinctly Old West feel. For fans of gunslinging women and young girl assassins. And dogs.

Under Falling Skies, the first book in *The Travels of Scout Shannon,* available everywhere now.

SCI-FI SERIAL PODCAST!

Check out my new monthly podcast of serialized science fiction: THE TALES OF THE CHAI MAKHANI TRIO!

Elyot loathes the massive Commonwealth ships that hover menacingly over his home world of Adghal. He hates the Commonwealth enforcers who harass the populace even more. But with his mother missing and presumed dead, Elyot keeps his head down and strives to avoid notice. And he succeeds until the day two strangers enter his life...

New episodes of this sci-fi serial drop every 1st of the month.

Now streaming on all major podcast platforms. Also available in eBook and print everywhere books or sold. For a complete episode listing, check out the page on my website.

ALSO FROM RATATOSKR PRESS

Also from Ratatoskr Press, *The Witches Three Cozy Mystery Series* by Cate Martin, a mix of mystery and magic that begins with Book 1: *Charm School.*

Amanda Clarke thinks of herself as perfectly ordinary in every way. Just a small-town girl who serves breakfast all day in a little diner nestled next to the highway, nothing but dairy farms for miles around. She fits in there.

But then an old woman she never met dies, and Amanda was named in her will. Now Amanda packs a bag and heads to the big city, to Miss Zenobia Weekes' Charm School for Exceptional Young Ladies. And it's not in just any neighborhood. No, she finds herself on Summit Avenue in St. Paul, a street lined with gorgeous old houses, the former homes of lumber barons, railroad millionaires, even the writer F. Scott Fitzgerald. Why, Amanda can practically hear the jazz music still playing across the decades.

Scratch that. The music really, literally, still plays in the backyard of the charm school. Because the house stretches across time itself. Without a witch to protect this tear in the fabric of the world, anything can spill over. Like music.

Or like murder.

The complete series is out now, and it all starts with *Charm School*.

FREE EBOOK!

Like exclusive, free content?

To get two prequel short stories to THE RITCHIE AND FITZ SCI-FI MURDER MYSTERIES as well as a bonus prequel novelette to the completed six-book series THE TRAVELS OF SCOUT SHANNON, signup for my monthly newsletter at KateMacLeodWrites.com.

Thank you!

ABOUT THE AUTHOR

Photograph © 2016 Jonathan Conklin

Kate MacLeod has written stories which have appeared in *Analog*, *Strange Horizons* and *Mythic Delirium*, among other places. She is also the author of two young adult science fictions series: *The Travels of Scout Shannon*, and *The Ritchie and Fitz Sci-Fi Murder Mysteries*. She also contributes to a serialized science fiction podcast called *The Tales of the Chai Makhani Trio*. She currently lives in Minneapolis, Minnesota.

Find out more about the author and sign up for her newsletter at KateMacLeodWrites.com.

ALSO BY KATE MACLEOD

Novels

The Slums of the Solar System:

Mitwa

The Mars of Malcontents

The Whole World for Each

Books 1-3 Box Set

The Travels of Scout Shannon:

Under Falling Skies

In Quaking Hills

Among Treacherous Stars

Against Impassable Barriers

Over Freezing Altitudes

At Galactic Central

The Travels of Scout Shannon Books 1-3

The Travels of Scout Shannon Books 4-6

The Travels of Scout Shannon Books 1-6

The Ritchie and Fitz Sci-Fi Murder Mysteries:

Murder on the Intergalactic Railway

Murder in the Skies

Body in the Catacombs

Death on the Summit

An Undiplomatic Murder

A Lethal Betrayal

The Forgotten Planet

Raiding the Forgotten Derelict (Forthcoming September 2024)

Sci-Fi Novellas

The Intergenerational Tree

I Rise into a Daybreak

Caper Novellas

The Third Pole Job

The Twelve Days of Christmas Job

10-Story Collections

Tales of Blood and Ink

Tales of Old Gods and New

5-Story Collections

Tales from Heian-Kyo and Others

Tales from the Edges and Ends

Tales from Forgotten Days

Tales from Ancient and Future Times

Tales from Across Space